DADDY'S MONEY

Vicki Baylis

ISBN 978-1-64140-283-5 (paperback)
ISBN 978-1-64140-284-2 (digital)

Christian Faith Publishing, Inc.
832 Park Avenue
Meadville, PA 16335
www.christianfaithpublishing.com

Printed in the United States of America

With a lifetime of memories and a heart filled with love, it is with overflowing happiness that I dedicate this book to my family—Chris, Eli, and Rebekah.

ACKNOWLEDGMENTS

Life on a farm is never-ending, from sunup to sundown, seven days a week through every season, day and night. And with every season brings its own challenges—snow, summer heat, wind, and rain. And with each challenge, God always sent someone to help and guide us through it. I thank all who helped give my children a lifetime of memories: chasing lizards, hunting, fishing, hanging with pawpaw, riding the tractor, feeding the animals, planting vegetables, riding the goats, baling hay, learning to drive a truck, scary cows, gathering the eggs, hanging with dad, stepping in cow patties, and playing in the hay.

To our banker, Tommy Fairley, for giving us the chance to be farmers.

To my uncles, Ben and Sam Perkins, who saw I needed an attic floor before I did and built it.

To my husband's father, Clifford, and his brother, Davey, who helped my husband live his dream.

To my neighbors, Mr. and Mrs. Wilson, who endured countless hours of questions without laughing hysterically.

To Wade Walker, who helped me learn how to vaccinate cows—oh, what fun that was.

To Charles Albert Walker, for the numerous times you fixed our tractor and hay balers when they were broken.

To Mr. and Mrs. Ward, who showed such strength when all my cows made a meal off their beautiful two-acre vegetable garden—we have since learned to build better fences.

To Dave Abel, who endured the countless hours and the painstaking task of proofreading all my stories.

And lastly, to my very best friend, Cindy Lee, and that man she married, for always being one phone call away and for always getting packed and ready for whatever next adventure that comes our way.

CONTENTS

The Nanny

1

She was most uncomfortable with someone touching her face. Adding to this stress were all the people surrounding her during her fifteen minutes of fame. The flamboyant male assisting with her make up puzzled her mind. Why hadn't someone already told him how ridiculous he looked, dressed in those blue feathers? Where were his friends? She never fancied herself with television or the actors who entered the television sets each day. In her view, the noise coming from today's Hollywood crowd was contributing to the downfall of society.

She was also trying to keep up with the overly skinny young woman holding tightly to a clipboard. But between the makeup artist applying enough for four people and the instructions about what to do once on stage, her patience was wearing thin. Perhaps that is why she said what she did: "Young man, stop this instant and take a good look at yourself in that mirror. Why on earth are you wearing those ridiculous feathers?"

Several onlookers gasped with surprise. But truth be known, they too were wondering. Somehow, in today's world of political correctness, observations of this nature were best not voiced for fear of being sued or, worse, being portrayed as a bigot. This was certainly never the intentions of Eleanor Sims. Instead, she had an innate ability to see through the eyes of those in pain and those who just needed an ear to listen. Mrs. Eleanor Sims, age sixty-eight, was known for speaking her mind, and this young man would be no exception.

After regaining his composure, he tried to act unbothered by her statement. In front of the few remaining staff members, who could not step away due to their jobs, he responded, "I'm expressing myself." And he began fluffing the colorful feathers that covered his neckline.

"Then tell me, young man," she asked, "what exactly are you trying to express?"

"Don't you get it? I'm gay." He continued to act as if she was the one with the problem.

"I see," she said with a little nod.

They were interrupted once again by the woman holding the clipboard who was holding up five fingers, implying five more minutes, so Eleanor assumed.

Eleanor turned and continued her conversation with the man who was standing in front of her, as if he were daring her to continue talking. Eleanor never bowed down when she felt the person really needed honesty, and this young man needed all she had.

"Young man"—she paused—"if you put the feathers on me, would you think I am gay?"

He opened his mouth to speak words he had already rehearsed many times in his head but realized they did not address the question. He stepped back, somewhat taken by her simple yet meaningful thought.

She continued, "My point is, dear, the feathers make you look like nothing more than a schoolchild playing dress up."

With slightly slumped shoulders, he returned the makeup to the counter then removed the plastic covering from around her neck. She gently patted his arm before being assisted out of the chair to go onstage. Those within earshot were desperately trying to hear what Eleanor was saying, but to no avail. Their brief conversation would remain between them and only them. Once again, she had been correct in her observation of a young man coming to terms with his life struggles.

The lights were more blinding and the crowd's applause a little louder than she had imagined, as she made her way to the host of the show, who stood up waiting to greet her as she approached. She smiled sweetly as she passed by little Timmy and his slightly older sister, Margaret-Anne Bohannon. Seated next to the children were their parents. Dr. Cliff Bohannon rose to gently embrace the woman who had single-handedly turned his family situation around during the previous year.

"Welcome, welcome to the show." The gracious host extended her arms to hug Eleanor.

"Thank you," the nervous guest responded as she took her seat.

The children could not contain their excitement any longer and sprang from the couch they shared with their parents to hug her as she settled into her chair.

"I missed you, Mrs. Eleanor," Timmy said, echoed by his sister, "Me too, me too."

The audience once again began to clap.

"Oh my, you two have grown a foot since I last saw you. What have you been eating?" Eleanor asked the children.

"Carrots and beans," Timmy blurted out.

The audience laughed at the honesty of the child. A very pregnant Mrs. Bohannon nudged the children back to their seats. The host began recalling some of the facts that led this everyday nanny to her recent spotlight.

"Let's take a look at the Bohannon story," the host announced.

The oversized viewer located to the right of the family began to display the story of how Eleanor Sims entered this very overworked and disorganized family. Dr. Bohannon had heard of her remarkable skills from a wealthy patient, whose nephew had retained her services two years earlier. The story began when Margaret-Anne was expelled from Westchester School for Young Ladies, a wealthy private school located outside Charleston, South Carolina. If your name was not on the waiting list practically within minutes after birth, chances were you did not get into this prestigious school. The children were in and out of day care and private nannies since birth. Lauren Bohannon had worked for the real estate giant, Brookes and Brady, for fourteen years before the birth of Margaret-Anne. She and the doctor delayed rearing children until her thirties. Sadly, by the time Eleanor came into this family, the children were uncontrollable, and the Bohannon marriage was on the brink of divorce.

"As everyone can see, life at this house was awful, and I do mean awful," the host jokingly said, as she made her way into the audience to begin the question-and-answer session.

Margaret-Anne handed her mother a tissue to wipe the escaping tears falling from her eyes. The doctor gently placed his arm around his wife.

Questions poured from members of the audience. Eleanor was firm with her answers, even when some disagreed with her methods, especially on the subject of stay-at-home-moms.

Mrs. Bohannon was quick to point out, "Quitting my job was the best thing I have ever done. I wouldn't change that now for anything."

Eleanor added that these kids, based on her observations, needed their mother at home, adding that it wasn't the case with all the families she had helped over the many years. Several in the audience asked for her services, but she had to decline.

"I've agreed to meet with a family next week," Eleanor stated.

Once the ordeal was over, she quickly darted offstage. Of course, the children were clinging to her side for they did not want her to leave. As she picked Timmy up, she noticed the makeup artist had changed clothing, now sporting a more casual look in faded jeans and a tight-fitted T-shirt. A handsome man indeed, she noted. She returned his wink with a smile and a nod of affirmation.

The woman with the clipboard noticed the feathers were gone and leaned over to ask, "What did she say to you anyway?"

He just smiled and shook his head.

The Assignment 2

The limo ride to the Windham Estates took her by surprise. The view of the ocean was breathtaking. If the size of the estate was any indication, this would be her wealthiest family yet. Up until this assignment, her salary had remained the same, regardless of the family income. She did have to admit this offer of employment changed the plans of her long-awaited retirement. In her wildest imagination, she could not fathom what would warrant a father to offer a half-million dollars for her services. But for that amount of money, she certainly could postpone her retirement six short months.

She thought, *Just how bad could this kid be?*

The long black limo had picked her up from the train station and now made its way along the circular driveway, stopping directly in front of the entrance to the mansion. Eleanor took in the beauty of the perfectly landscaped yard. Nothing was out of place. The yard, the most beautiful sea of deep lush green, seemed to go on forever. Before the driver departed his seat, a distinguished-looking gray-haired man, dressed appropriately for the position of butler, stepped through the massive doors, which she presumed led into a grand foyer of wealthy proportions.

"Welcome, Mrs. Sims," he said as the driver opened the car door.

The woman was not accustomed to butlers and chauffeurs, as was evident by the grin on her face.

"Oh, thank you," she said, as they both grabbed for her overnight bag.

13

"Right this way, Mrs. Sims." He proceeded into the foyer. It was just as she had imagined it would be.

Feeling slightly underdressed, she, for the first time, noticed the wrinkle in her skirt.

"Oh dear!" she mumbled to herself, trying desperately to smooth the wrinkle with her hand.

"I beg your pardon, madam?" the butler asked.

"Oh, oh. Nothing," she replied.

Why was she so nervous? Never in all her days had she been nervous before an interview. Was it the money? Was it the mansion? Just what was her gut instinct trying to tell her? She sat patiently, waiting for the self-made millionaire to enter the room. She could not help eavesdropping on his conversation taking place right outside the study doorway: "Then go, get him up, right now! I don't care what you have to do, just get him here at twelve."

The slender man walked confidently into the room, pausing in front of Eleanor, gently shaking her hand. "Thank you so much for coming. My associates are big fans of the *Jackie Raney Show* and knew immediately we needed your help with Jon Marcus. I take full responsibility for the way he turned out."

He never wasted time beating around the bush, as was evident in the way he got right to the point.

"His mother, Rachel, God rest her soul, passed away shortly after giving birth, and I didn't have time to raise a child. My business was branching out, and I was traveling a lot, months at a time. I hastily hired the first person interviewed, looking back, probably not one of the best moves, but I was dumb as a rock when it came to child-rearing. Rachel was more down-to-earth. She would have made a wonderful mother." He paused, as if a memory from the past flooded his soul.

"One of the reasons I loved her so much, so down-to-earth," he repeated, "so easy to talk to."

He paused again briefly and shook his head, as if trying to keep the memory at bay.

"She had a special knack for helping people and would have made a wonderful mother. Did I say that already? Forgive me." He returned the framed picture of his late wife to its place on his desk.

"After a while, I found comfort in the first pretty young thing I found. I was lonely, overworked, and overwhelmed with that boy. I should have known better, but one sees what one wants to. I guess I thought he would outgrow being spoiled. My second wife, Amanda, was more into shopping and the country club than into raising a child. She was just so young. Jon Marcus grew up without proper discipline. Again, I cannot fault him solely. I blame myself."

"We all fall short, Mr. Howell," Eleanor responded. "It is never too late to turn the young man around. Where is the lad now? In school?"

Mr. Howell, who had been standing, gazing out the window, turned around to answer. "Mrs. Sims"—he paused, not knowing exactly how to say it—"I thought my secretary informed you about the situation."

Upon learning the age of the child in question, Eleanor Sims made a beeline for the door. Had this man lost his mind? She did not intend to be a nanny to a grown man. And out the door, she went.

"Good Lord! Where is that car?" She did not even look back when the butler called her name. *Never in my born days*, she said to herself, as she strolled quickly down the driveway, slinging the overnight bag in one hand and her purse in the other.

The Plan   3

Jonathan Marcus Howell II was a thorn in his father's side. Money meant nothing to him, except for the fact it was necessary and certainly always available when he needed it. Many attempts failed, trying to teach him budgeting. The accountants and secretaries hired to help always ended up as disposable girlfriends or enemies of the family soon after employment and, not to mention, a few sexual harassment complaints, which were always stopped short of any legal tarnishes to the family name. It was far less of a headache for everyone involved to pay the bills for him. Although he had been schooled at the best facilities money could afford, Jon Marcus learned more about girls and jet setting than anything else. The headmaster was just as eager to take Mr. Howell's donations as he was to get the troublemaker out of his prestigious school. J. Marcus Howell Sr. paid for his son's education. College never even crossed the family's mind. All this young lad was interested in was partying. In fact, on any given day, this twenty-two-year-old would still be in bed, along with whatever thing the cat had dragged in the previous night. However, today, the hotel staff would awaken him. Under direct orders from the owner of Bay Harbor Inn, regardless of whatever it took, Jon Marcus would be at his father's estate precisely at noon.

$$\$\$\$$$

The golf cart, going at full speed, barely caught up to the fuming woman. She was waiting for the entrance gate to open. This man had wasted her time, not to mention, delayed her retirement plans.

16

"Mrs. Sims, please wait. Mrs. Sims, please!" he pleaded from the fast-approaching cart.

"Mr. Howell, I'm afraid there is nothing you could say to convince me to stay."

Eleanor had done a lot of things in her lifetime and not once turned away from an assignment for fear it would be too hard. In fact, it was the most difficult children that tugged at her heartstrings the most. But this child was not a child at all. He was a grown man. She finished her sentence and looked directly into the face of Mr. Howell. He paused as if he was having trouble admitting what was on his mind, but she had made her mind up, and nothing he could say would be enough to change it. She waited patiently as he regained his composure. "I'm dying, Mrs. Sims."

She did not see that coming.

"I have six months to a year if I'm lucky. I have to fix this terrible mistake. He will inherit a good deal of money, but without fixing the problem, he will go through it in no time. Then what? What will he do then? It keeps me up at night worrying about this." He paused to catch his breath. "I don't know what else to do. I am desperate, Mrs. Sims. I'll pay you one million. Just please help him. Please."

And for the first time, she could see his desperation. The entrance gate swung opened. Hating herself, she turned away and began to walk through it.

Believing he had failed to convince the woman, whom he looked upon as his last chance, he turned the cart around and headed back to his home. From the steps of the mansion, the butler and the housekeeper were anxiously waiting to see the outcome.

And it was with heavy sighs, Eleanor stopped her departure and said, "Mr. Howell, it must be done my way and only my way."

Eleanor accepted the challenge, perhaps her greatest challenge yet.

$$$

Lunch was being served on the patio overlooking the ocean. Everyone knew from the sounds of the squealing tires approaching the home that "he" had arrived. Within minutes, the front door slammed.

"Where are you?" the frustrated young man screamed in effort to hurry his father. "I don't have all day!" he shouted again.

Under Eleanor's instruction, Mr. Howell remained seated at the meal. Everyone, staff included, needed to be retrained in dealing with this man.

"If you don't hurry, I'm leaving."

The two of them continued to eat. The housekeeper's hands became shaky while refilling the tea glasses.

"Housekeeper!" he rudely shouted. "Where is my father?"

Jon Marcus was storming through the grand room when he noticed the two of them sitting on the patio.

"Cold water. I had cold water poured on my head. On my head!" the young man shouted.

His temper was clearly affecting his ability to sound rational as he finally pointed to his head still wet.

Mr. Howell motioned for his son to join them for lunch.

"I'm not hungry. Who's she?" Jon Marcus's rudeness continued to shine vividly as his father motioned again for him to join them at the table.

Mr. Howell had been fully instructed on how to handle step one. Until the son calmed down and began to eat, not one word was to be spoken between them about the new plan.

He glared at his father but refused to sit down. Not having his questions answered only made the young man more furious, and he stormed off.

"Step one, Mr. Howell, step one." She was slightly pleased, even showing a little smile, as she continued on with her meal.

$$$

His afternoon usually included his favorite sport of tennis at the country club. If his stepmother taught him anything, it was how to get the most out of his father's money. At the club, one did not need to carry cash, checks, or even credit cards for that matter. The continuously running tab was all that was needed—a tab that an accountant somewhere in one of his father's many offices paid on a monthly basis. He parked the little red sports car, as always, in the handicap space. Many times, the management threatened him with towing, but he did not care. It was a tennis club after all, and someone with a wheelchair couldn't play tennis—his theory, which he shared numerous times in his defense. He signed in at the front desk and headed to the courts. He was surprised to find his reserved court was being used.

"Hey, what's going on?" He opened the gate door and proceeded onto the court.

The older women, having a group lesson, immediately stopped their game of tennis. Jon Marcus stood dumbfounded when the tennis pro informed him of his cancelled membership. Of course, he demanded to see the office manager. The ladies gasped at the ill-manners of the young man venting his complaints to the instructor.

The courts fell silent. A few of the other instructors came to aid in any way they could. Everyone was watching. And when the angry man tripped over his own tennis bag, everyone laughed.

Truthfully, the instructor was glad to see him finally get thrown out of the club, as was evident by the grin that he tried but failed to hide from the women standing around him. He did his best to get the ladies back on track, but because they were giggling at the excitement they had just witnessed, accompanied by the instructor's grinning, it was useless. Finally, he gave in to the giggles himself.

"Cynthia Kincade, may I help you?" The new office manager approached him at the doorway. She had been expecting his fireworks. Although new to the club, she had been fully warned of the youngest Howell. Grandfather Shelton McIntyre Howell III had not only been a founding member but also owner, going to the club every day since opening. The aging tennis pro resided at the exclusive Westchester Estates until passing from complications of a stroke. Many believed he gave up longing to play the game one more time. His days at the club were not only joyful but also filled with years of hard work. Shelton had poured every ounce of money he earned into his dream of giving his family more than he had.

"What's going on? I have been a member here since birth. Do you know who my father is?" Jon Marcus ranted.

"Well, I know your father has been a member here for years, but I cannot find any record of you." Miss Kincade remained calm and professional.

"Duh, I'm on his account," Jon Marcus continued with his famous sarcastic tone.

"Well, duh. Anyone over the age of twenty-one must have his or her own account. Refer to section fourteen of the club rules." She paused. "Shall I open you an account?"

"Whatever!" he said, rolling his eyes.

"Great. Step into my office, please. It's twenty-five hundred to open an account, and three hundred up front for the first month dues."

"Whatever!" He scribbled his name and then tossed a credit card onto her desk. She appeared to have trouble scanning the card and needed to call the number to its customer service. All the while, he appeared bored with the entire process; after all, he needed to get a game in before the afternoon rain.

"Mr. Howell, there appears to be a problem with your card," said the manager.

"Just swipe it through your little machine. It's not rocket science, you know." Jon was past the point of being aggravated with the entire process.

"Obviously, but your card has been cancelled," she replied, pleased to get the last laugh.

He sighed heavily and said, "Here, do this one." Aggravated, he handed her another one. With the first swipe, the machine read "Declined."

"This one is declined also, Mr. Howell."

He stood up to protest. "Obviously, you're doing it wrong. Here, let me do it."

Swipe two—the card declined. The power flickered about the same time as the thunder sounded.

"Now see what you've done. Now it is raining. Game over."

"Mr. Howell"—she paused and stood up—"the weather is certainly not in my job description, but if you would like, I'll try to get

Mother Nature on the phone for you." She had had about all she was going to take from this man.

"Whatever." He left the room, grabbing the cards from her extended hand.

The tow truck was exiting the club parking lot just as he walked through the entrance door.

"Wait!" His attempt to catch the moving vehicle had failed, leaving him soaked by the fast-moving downpour that appeared from out of the sky as he chased the tow truck. His tantrum only sealed his fate. For now, no one at the club was willing to take the soaked man home.

"Shall I call you a cab, sir?" offered the door attendant.

$$$

Thanks to the call from a long-time friend at the country club, Eleanor and her new boss knew it would be only a matter of minutes before the young man would realize he had also been evicted from his suite at Bay Harbor Inn. The sweet young thing that stayed over from the previous night was throwing tantrum herself as she was being physically removed from her leisurely afternoon bubble bath. By the time Jon Marcus made his way up to his room, she was wrapped in the complimentary hotel robe, sitting on one of his suitcases, drinking the last of whatever she could find left over from last night's drinking binge.

"What are you doing?" He insisted on an explanation as to why his personal belongings were in the hallway.

She threw up her arms and motioned toward the door. A few of the staff members were packing up his things.

"Ask them. And get my clothes!"

$$$

He stood in the middle of the room dripping the remaining wetness from his soaked clothing onto the white marble flooring. The housekeeper rushed to the laundry room to retrieve towels. Eleanor and his father were sitting on the sofa. As with all her clients, she studied old photos in order to get a true sense of the individual's character. Little childhood faces usually revealed truths. They had been discussing his love of animals as a youngster, his father regretting the need to give up his pets. His stepmother's severe allergies only caused tension in the already stressed environment.

"Would somebody please tell me what is going on?" Jon Marcus demanded.

"Son, this is Mrs. Eleanor Sims," his father started to say.

"Not her. I'm talking about me. My car, my credit cards, the hotel." His voice was a little shaken due to the events unfolding in his life over the course of a few hours. "What is going on?" Jon Marcus insisted on knowing.

"Why don't you calm down and go change into something dry," the father suggested.

The housekeeper had just arrived with the towels and a change of clothes.

Only One Option 4

He returned to the grand room dry, but that was the only change. He was still sullen like a toddler. His father once again tried to introduce Eleanor, but the young man would have no part with formalities.

"Just tell me what's going on," he demanded.

His father made several attempts to get started, but each time failed. This man—a man who had no problems running a multi-million dollar enterprise that he had single-handedly started from the ground up—found himself for the first time in his life at a loss for words. He was actually relieved when the housekeeper reported dinner was ready.

"Mrs. Sims, perhaps it will be better coming from you." Thorough details were given over the course of the meal. Jon Marcus showed no emotion one way or the other, as if the conversation did not pertain to him at all.

"Son, do you understand? I'm trying to help you."

The young man showed the first sign of manners when he carefully wiped the corners of his mouth, then he stood up to leave the room.

Eleanor stood also. "Sit down!"

Her reaction not only stopped his exit but also startled the father.

"Did I hear you correctly?" inquired the young man. The challenge was on. This would be where the father would learn exactly what one million dollars was paying for.

"Let me begin to tell you what is going to happen." Her voice, although not loud or demeaning in any way, demanded attention. She walked over to the young man and looked at him face-to-face. "Your father has already written a new will. Your name is not included. All your credit cards have been cancelled, and all bank accounts have been deleted. You are actually homeless as we speak. That little sports car has been sold. Your next meal will be up to you." She paused to let things set in. "Are we clear so far?"

He stood quietly for a moment then walked over to his father, saying, "You're not serious?"

His father, a little relieved the situation had been explained, said, "It's going to help you, son."

Nevertheless, the son could not understand.

"I think I know what's going on here." He leaned down to whisper into his father's ear, "You're being blackmailed, aren't you?"

"No, son. This is going to help. Don't fight it," the father pleaded.

"I'd like to discuss a few things with you, Jon Marcus," Eleanor interrupted. However, the angry young man wanted no part of this nonsense and left slamming the door behind him. His new course of bad luck continued as the rain began to fall once more.

Eleanor and Mr. Howell watched as he walked off into the downpour.

"Step two, sir, step two," she said as she gently patted his shoulder. "We're getting there, but you and I have lots of work to do. Let's get started, shall we?" She paused and then asked, "Do you still have that land down south?"

Jon Marcus walked out the entrance gate, all the while trying to dial his cell phone. Once he realized the phone was dead, he threw it as far as he could, cursing as loudly as his voice would go.

Johnny Was the Farmer   5

A week had passed since his new life had started. His so-called friends were one by one tired of him and becoming increasingly busy without him. He awakened to the sounds of children playing in the background. The occasional barking of dogs in the distance appeared to be getting closer with each passing bark. The bright sunlight proved to be too much for the hangover his head was experiencing this morning. Details of the previous night were vague, to say the least. His attempt to sit upright on the park bench was interrupted by the police officer trying to get his attention with a billy club.

"What?" he yelled at the officer.

It appeared to Jon Marcus that already the day was going downhill fast. He was leaning back on the park bench, holding his newly obtained ticket when the stranger approached him.

"What you got there, son?"

Although he tried, the sunlight blocked any attempt to reveal the stranger's identity.

"Apparently, it's against the law to sleep on this bench."

He stood up and shouted toward the officer who was still within sight, "The very bench I paid for with my taxes!"

As Jon Marcus shouted, the officer kept walking, disregarding the man's ill judgment.

The stranger offered, "How about some breakfast?" as he pointed to the café within eyesight.

As the two of them finished their meal, the man pulled two envelopes from his brief case.

25

Jon Marcus looked up, saying, "What's that?"

However, the stranger said nothing, only sliding from the booth and darting out the nearest exit. Soon, he gave in to curiosity and opened the first letter, noting his father's handwriting. The note read:

Dear son,

This is the hardest thing I have ever done. Please know I am doing it because I love you dearly. I wish your mother could have stayed with us longer. You would have truly loved her. All who knew her envied her gentleness and caring nature. When you were just a toddler, I knew you inherited those wonderful qualities also. I regret I forced you to grow up fast and without proper instructions. The boarding school changed you, and I am deeply troubled that I forced you to go. It is too late to change some things, but I truly believe that you are still young enough to regain some of what I took away. Before your mother passed away, she was making plans to move us to a more peaceful place, away from all the chaos of city life. When I married your stepmother, she would have no part of country life, and that is why we built here. I now ache for your mother's dream. I regret I took that from you. Enclosed are pictures of the only vacation we took together before Amanda entered our life. It is one of my fondest memories. You may have forgotten, but once, you adored animals. It is why I am doing this. I want you to get back to the way you were before me and your stepmother ruined things. I love you, son, and this is my way of making things right. I have put the house on the market and have already gotten a good offer. I plan to travel this old world and get myself back to the

man your mother loved. Here is my gift to you.
Good luck, my son. I will see you when I return.

PS: Mrs. Sims will be there to help you. She is
really a great and knowledgeable woman.

For the moment, he seemed to be consumed with the pictures.
Perhaps there was a brief smile or two upon the saddened face—so
brief the naked eye might miss. The pictures were unfamiliar to him.
Sure, he recognized himself. There were many portraits around the
mansion depicting the happiness a family who had everything must
be enjoying. However, he could not remember the animals or the
infant he was holding. The caption on the back of the pictures only
stated "Brinson's farm. 1982." He could not recall anyone named
Brinson or any of the happiness that was so apparent on the little
boy's face. In fact, he could not recall a time when his father looked
so carefree.

The second envelope contained a typed letter, a bus ticket, and
250 dollars. It stated the following:

Jon Marcus,
I will be expecting you to arrive by Friday.
That will give you a couple of days to say your
goodbyes and travel. Your personal belongings
have already been shipped, and I have taken the
liberty to pack you a few changes of clothes. Ask
your waitress for your suitcase. It is behind the
counter.
And now, are you ready for some good
news? Your father has instructed me to give you
your full inheritance in one year. There is one
stipulation: you have been given farmland down
south. It is there that you will reside for the entire
time. In order to get the inheritance, the farm
must become self-sufficient at the end of the first
year. If not, you will not get any of the money;

instead, it will be donated to a charity of your father's choice. Here are a few rules that must be followed. Any breach in these rules, and you forfeit the money:

1. No one is to know your background. As far as everyone is concerned, you are just a city boy who wants to move to the country.
2. No smoking/no alcohol. By the way, the farm is located in a dry county. That means no one sells alcohol anyway.
3. A job has been selected for you in town. That's right. A job! If you do not work, you do not eat.
4. It is equally important that you attend the church of your choice at least three times a week. That is both sermons on Sunday and Wednesday night prayer meeting. Henry Pope, a farmer, will help you with the farm. *Help* is the key word; not do it for you. His wife, Esther, will be around to lend a hand also. Your father has placed money at the local bank to take care of their salary for the entire year and to help with any repairs that the farm needs. This farm is yours, and you can do with it whatever you like with it, except sell it. Just remember, it must be self-sufficient.

$$$

He sat quietly, ignoring the hustling servers as they continued to earn their living within the walls of the café. He did not even flinch when the busboy dropped a bucket of dirty dishes. His mind was in deep thought—*twelve months, 365 days*. He could handle that. In fact, that would be a mere picnic compared to the years shipped off to boarding schools. He sat there alone, arms clasped together behind his head, again in deep thought. He had to admit this would not be the hardest thing he ever faced. It would be twelve short months until the freedom of no more trust funds and no more of his father's accountants telling him how to live and what to do and what not to do. He would accept Eleanor's challenge. After all, he had beaten the best that Ivy League schools could produce, referring to the mounds of people hired to tame him. Surely, this Mrs. Sims, as simple-minded individual as she was, would soon fail like the others.

The Train Rides Back in Time 6

No amount of talking could convince Eleanor to let him take the company jet to New Orleans. He had planned everything down to the minute, all the while taking several hours off the entire dreaded trip. He would rent a car at the airport and drive the remainder of the way. Eleanor stood her ground, though. The train ride was not the issue at hand but rather getting the point across to the young man who was in charge.

The long journey was planned in such a way as to give the young man time to relax and gather ideas from each passing farm along the way. Eleanor knew this would be her hardest case to date—definitely surpassing the McGuire twins and, she believed, even worse than Tiffany Delaney, the Texas socialite, who suffered paralysis in an auto accident shortly after being crowned Homecoming Queen. If everything worked out, the young man would have many ideas for his farmland whether he knew it or not.

$$\$\$\$$$

The train pulled into the Hattiesburg depot shortly before midnight. Henry Pope, a farmer, was sitting on the small wooden bench located outside the ticket office. He was whittling on a piece of wood. Eleanor insisted he would have no trouble spotting the young man, and once again, she had proven to be right. Henry and his wife, Esther, had known Eleanor Sims for many years and had personally seen with their own eyes the miracles she worked on children.

The tinted spiked hair was a dead giveaway, not to mention his clothes. Henry nearly choked about on the cola he had been sipping when the city slicker exited the train.

"Oh yeah. He's going to fit right in," Henry said to himself and giggled a little.

As predicted, the new farmer-to-be was tired and, to Henry's surprise, intoxicated; but the young man would have nothing to do with delaying the trip until morning.

"Son, Eleanor has rooms reserved for us here in town for tonight," Henry tried again.

"No way am I adding another day to this nightmare."

"But the farm doesn't even have power or water turned on yet," he was trying again to convince the young man it would be best to spend the night in town.

"Don't need any lights to sleep," he argued.

"Suit yourself, son. It'll take us another couple of hours to get there."

"You lead. I'll follow," Jon Marcus said as he tried desperately to walk a straight line but couldn't.

"Well, all righty then," Henry added as he tossed the empty Coke bottle into the trash can and began to walk to his truck.

$$$

When morning came, it was hard to tell who was more scared: the rooster resting on the headboard crowing above his head, or the frightened young man surrounded by the biggest cats known to humanity. His screaming alerted everyone that the sleeping beauty was awake. He fell through the opening that once housed a door. Although words were coming out, they were hard to understand.

"Ca, cas, cats!"

"Yeah, Esther put them in there to get rid of the rats. Those things must weigh twenty pounds each by now."

"Rats?" he yelled.

"I told you the place wasn't ready to live in yet."

"No! No! No! You said it didn't have water!" he exclaimed, angry to be the butt of Henry's laughing.

"Son, you got a little something right there." Henry pointed to the forehead.

"What the?" He was dumbfounded at the brownish liquid that now also was on his finger. And upon his further inspection, it was all over him too.

"Hmm, I believe that would be chicken poop." Eleanor seemed tickled to report.

In fact, the entire night's sleep had been in the room the chickens viewed as their own. Once he noticed he was covered, head to toe, with their droppings, he stripped down to his fancy under briefs.

"I need a shower and coffee!" he yelled, pacing back and forth trying to locate anything that looked like water.

Eleanor came to the rescue. It would be the first of many, many times to come. She pointed down the road to the recreational vehicle sitting under the oak trees.

"Oh, thank God!" he said as he made a fast trip down the gravel road.

Well, he was as fast as a man with tender feet could make—two steps and then a few choice words, a pause, and then two steps, and another round of words.

"Oh yeah, this is gonna be fun," Henry exclaimed.

The droppings would soon prove to be the lesser of the problems associated with sleeping with chickens.

$$$

Henry drove them both to town with Eleanor up front and Jon Marcus, riding solo outside in the bed of the truck. The doctor's office was not busy, and they would be able to see him as soon as they arrived. Henry began to giggle.

"Henry, stop laughing at the boy this instance. The poor child has just about scratched his skin off," she protested but, all the while, admitting it was funny.

"Yeah, but I've never seen chicken mites react so badly to someone."

The country doctor was well loved by everyone in the town. If you were born after 1980, chances were he helped bring you into this world. His office looked more like a country home than a medical facility. Mrs. Evie Rogers greeted the poor soul at the front door.

"Come on back, honey, and don't be touching anything. There's a paper gown on the table," she instructed.

There was one thing for sure about Evie Rogers, and that was she ran a tight ship. There was no wasted time in her world, and cleanliness was next to godliness.

"Let me get a chart started on you, son. Name?"

"Jon Smith." Changing his last name was Eleanor's suggestion.

"Birthday?"

"June 15, 1982." That was another lie.

"Address?"

"I believe it's called hell."

"Don't be smart with me, young man."

"Can you stop this itching?" he demanded.

"First things first. Address?"

"Don't know it."

"What do you mean you don't know it? Are you special, honey?"

He had no idea what she was asking.

"You know, handicapped?"

"I am itching! Make it stop!"

"How come you don't know your address? I need an address before we can go any further." She was a stickler for rules.

He bolted from the table, pushed open the waiting room door, and marched over to Eleanor. "Where do I live?" he stated, pausing between each word, revealing his true frustration.

Eleanor jotted down the new address. As he turned, heading back toward the door, he became increasingly aware that the backside of his gown was revealing more than needed to be seen. It was at that time he noticed the brown-haired beauty sitting at the receptionist desk.

Soon, the doctor came in. Somewhere between the shot and the cream, the itching became bearable. Evie decided his clothing needed discarding and gave him another paper gown to drape across his backside for the trip home.

"That's some scar you got there, young man," Evie commented on the inch-long scar located on his lower back, as she helped tie the gown together.

Jon Marcus would have no part in the idle chitchat so common to people from the south. In fact, as soon as Evie tied the gown around his neck, he left without saying a word. Evie watched as the young man walked down the hallway leading to the waiting room. She remained in deep thought until interrupted by the doctor.

"What are you looking at?" The doctor stared down the hall.

"Do you know who that was?" she asked.

He looked down at the chart and said, "Yeah, Jon Smith. Why?"

"I think that's our Jon," Evie stated.

"Like, it was our Jon you thought you saw in Memphis and then again when we went to Florida? How about when you nearly got me arrested for following that kid around at Yellow Stone Park five years ago? Let it go, Evie. Let it go."

She knew the doctor was right. She had been wrong so many times when it came to Jon—their long-lost Jon.

"But he had the scar," she defended her intuitions.

"Every kid that comes in this place has scars, Evie. I don't want to hear anything else about it."

$$$

Evie's mind wandered back to the last day she saw her nephew. It had been a typical Saturday for a working mother of three. Her youngest child was lying on a quilt, watching her hang the last of the day's laundry on the clothesline. Her oldest two and her nephew were playing within earshot when the children began crying. The two-year-old had been hurt. A rusty nail had pierced his lower back, and Evie couldn't get it to stop bleeding. Even though Evie's father drove as fast as possible, the child was losing blood, and soon, it would be serious if they didn't get to the hospital. The ringing phone brought her back to the present, and soon, the thoughts of Jon vanished.

Day Two

7

The roosters crowed again, only this time waking the young man from the comfort of the truck. No amount of convincing could have talked the angry young man out of the air-conditioned cab last night. The purring of the diesel had drowned most of the sounds coming from the country nightlife, and with the exception of one bathroom break during the night, he slept through until morning. Jon Marcus had fallen asleep fearing defeat. But something about this morning proved to change his mind. How did he miss the beauty of the land yesterday? Perhaps it was the chaos from the morning's rude awakening. He had even missed it while he and Henry were emptying the old house of everything that was not nailed down. His bones were aching as he turned the engine off, but yesterday, he could have picked the truck up without thinking because he was so angry—angry at the chickens, the heat, the itching. Everything after the chicken mites that had made their presence known was a blur. He was standing off to the right side of the dilapidated house when Henry drove up.

"You look like you feel a little better this morning," Henry said, as he handed him one of Esther's homemade biscuits and a large cup of coffee.

"Look out there. I missed all this yesterday." Jon Marcus stood amazed at the pastureland in front of him. The sun was just rising into view.

"Yeah, this place was once one of the best in the county. One hundred head of cattle. The old man died in a nursing home."

"Cattle?" Jon inquired.

"Yep."

"Any money in it?"

"Some. If you do it right." Henry reached into the brown paper bag, grabbing them both another biscuit.

"Hey, look!" Jon Marcus had noticed a doe and her fawns off in the distance.

"Yep. The place is full of them."

"Any money in them?"

"No. Not really."

"Are there any bears out here?" Something unfamiliar had put him quickly back into the truck during the night.

"Don't believe. Was probably just a coyote."

Jon Marcus propped his foot on the barbed wire, just as Henry had done a few minutes earlier, and immediately found his fence post was rotten. Soon, it became obvious to both men that they would be heading back to the doctor's office on this morning.

$$$

"What now?" Nurse Rogers asked as she met them at the door.

"Might need a stitch or two. He got himself caught in the barbed wire," Henry informed the nurse.

"Get me his chart, Caroline," she instructed the young girl behind the counter, then she grabbed his lower arm, applying pressure to the wound with padded gauze. "Hurry on up. You're dripping blood all over the place."

She hurried him through the waiting room door and into the procedure room where Doctor Rogers was waiting. Eleanor had made a phone call while they were en route to the clinic.

"Evie, get me a tetanus," he instructed his nurse.

But as always, she was one step ahead and handed him the shot about the same time as he finished the sentence.

"Looks like stitches in this one," the doctor informed the patient.

$$$

36

Throughout the remainder of the day, technicians were making their way to the dilapidated farm. The pest control man was the first, followed by the plumber and then the electrician. The local lumberyard delivered the materials needed to patch the roof and replace the doors and windows. A carpenter was needed to repair many of the major problems. He and the roofer would be delayed a week. At four o'clock in the afternoon, the service technician from Hattiesburg rolled in to give an estimate on the new heating and air-conditioning system.

"Ed, Hardy Street Heating and Air," the technician said as he extended his hand.

"When can you start?" he asked.

"It shouldn't take my guys more than a day or two. When will the carpenters have the windows in?"

"Next week, but I'm ready for cold air now. It's like living in an oven around here."

"Now?"

"Yep."

He had heard Henry say this word many times, and he was sarcastically trying it.

"But you'll be cooling the world if the windows aren't in."

"Don't care."

"Well, I guess we can start in the morning."

"All righty then."

It was another of Henry's phrases the city boy was throwing out there for the first time.

$$$

With some satisfaction that he had gotten the ball rolling today, he walked the short piece down the gravel road—this time with shoes on—to Eleanor's RV. Esther had prepared supper, and the day's hard work had created a bear-sized appetite in both men. A couple of Tylenol and two helpings of supper were all his body could handle. With all the talk today about cows, Henry suggested getting the forty-acre pasture ready. Henry's question would go unanswered as everyone noticed the new farmer was sound asleep on the couch.

$$$

He awoke to the smell of bacon frying in the cast iron skillet.

"Biscuits about ready," Esther informed him, as he fixed himself a cup of coffee.

He moaned. Although he considered himself physically fit, he was now using muscles he did not know he had. Adding to this was the soreness from the barbed wire cuts.

"It'll get better as the day goes by. They'll work themselves out," Esther said, trying to help the young man's spirit.

He sat at the kitchen table staring off into space, his body too sore to think about the day's work ahead.

"Burning daylight, boy," Henry shouted through the screened door. "The chickens got back into the house again, and we're going to have to catch them before Ed and his crew will go in."

He threw his head back in aggravation at the thought of chasing chickens again. The idea made his skin itch just thinking about it. Eleanor entered the kitchen just in time to hear Henry's request.

"Ed, Ed, I don't know Ed," he thought aloud, eyes still focused on the ceiling.

Eleanor poured herself coffee and said, "Isn't Ed the air-conditioning guy?"

With those few words, Jon Marcus darted outside. Nothing was more precious to this young man than cool air, and Ed was bringing cool air.

While Ed and his boys worked with sheet metal and copper lines, the plumbers installed the toilet, sink, and shower into the bathroom. Jon, as he would now be referred to mainly because everyone kept calling him Mr. Marcus, began to appreciate the laborers' hard work.

By noon, the two men had mended the chicken coop and cleared the brush from the yard. After lunch, it would be Jon's turn to cut the forty acres on the right side of the house. The pasture needed to be ready before Saturday. That was when the stockyard would be open. Jon found himself wanting to buy cows. The guys working on the house had him pumped about which cows were the best breed, which ones produced the best milk, and, especially, which ones made the better profit. All this information only confused him more, and besides, Jon had some doubts about what the men were saying. He had already been the butt of many country boy jokes since they had arrived. But he was desperate to make a profit, and Junior, Lil Bill, and Leroy said cows meant profit.

Esther brought sandwiches, and the two men ate under one of the oak trees. Henry went over again the instructions about the tractor, just to be sure Jon understood. The plan was while Jon mowed, Henry would build the nest for the chickens to lay eggs. After Jon's fight with the roosters earlier in the day, he vowed never to touch the varmints again. The roosters are the reason Jon now carried a big stick everywhere he went.

Surprising to Jon, he actually enjoyed the tractor. It gave him a sense of importance sitting high on the big green machine. He had almost cleared the entire pasture of the overgrowth when he unintentionally ran over a nest of yellow jackets hidden in the ground. The men watched from the house as the unmanned tractor made its way through the field, making a big continuous circle while Jon headed toward the pond, swatting at the few remaining pests following right behind him.

$$$

Henry drove as fast as he could. As best as he could tell, Jon had been stung ten or so times.

Once again, Evie was waiting for him at the door. "Good Lord, son. What now?"

By now, he knew Evie's routine and grabbed the paper gown out of the drawer himself, as he walked to the exam room. This time, when the appointment was over, the young receptionist spoke as he went by, "See you tomorrow." Evie laughed. Jon did not.

They arrived home just as Ed was starting up the new air-conditioning system. He laid down next to the cooling vent on the floor of his unfinished home and soon went to sleep.

$$$

The sounds of drills and hammers woke the sleeping farmer. He lay there, arms still swollen from the yellow jackets, scabs still covering his body from the chicken mites, and—of course—the stitches from the barbed wire cuts were still annoying him, thinking, *Day four. Day four. I'm going to die here in this stupid backwoods country.*

To everyone's surprise, the carpenters arrived ahead of schedule. Finally, there was something good. It did not take the skilled laborers long to install the doors and windows. They were tearing out rotten boards faster than Jon could haul them off. Soon, the attic framework was in place. The carpenters covered the holes in the roof with plastic until the roofers could install the new one. Four o'clock in the afternoon came, and everyone poked fun at the tired young man. "You are dragging behind."

"Yeah, well."

"Just look how much work you can get done if you ain't wasting time at the doctor's office," Henry said jokingly.

"Yeah, well"—he paused at the sight of a truck coming down the gravel road—"I don't care who that is. I'm not working on anything else today."

In four short days, Jon had not only learned that bush hogging meant to mow the fields, he had actually gotten successful at driving the tractor too. He was nailing boards with a hammer, catching chickens, fighting roosters, and—basically—being the gofer for the plumber, electrician, and carpenters.

Evie Rogers pulled into the dirt driveway bringing homemade cookies. She rolled down the window and announced, "Since you didn't come in today, the doc sent me to check on you. Thought maybe you were dead or something."

Henry laughed.

"The place is looking better," said the off-duty nurse.

"Yeah, well, it's going slow. Going to the doctor every few minutes and all," Henry joked.

The two of them gave her the grand tour. She pointed out helpful hints that only a woman might notice, recalling things about the home she remembered from years past. They thanked her for the cookies, as she and Henry headed down the newly built steps. Jon was pointing out the fact he had helped build them earlier in the day when he jumped off the unscreened porch.

"Oh god!" Jon yelled in pain.

"Well, that looks like it should hurt." Evie pointed out.

"Son, you ever heard of 'look before you leap?'" Henry added as he was shaking his head in disbelief. Henry removed the board nailed to the bottom of Jon's right foot. "Henry, help me get him into the car. We better let doc take a look."

Evie and the doc met at the hospital when she was in nursing school and he was in his last year of residency. The two of them started up the clinic after they were married two years later and have been a top-notched team for thirty-four years.

$$\$\$\$$

It was a beautiful day for a sermon. The congregation listened ever so diligently as the weekly announcements were given. As with every Sunday, the pastor slowly scanned through the pews. Brother Johnson loved his members, and for the past thirty-four years, they loved him too. He noticed Sister Edna's seat remained vacant once more. It had been two months since her passing, and no one had the heart to fill it.

He silently praised God that her suffering had ended and that she was now rejoicing in Heaven. A few pews over from the empty seat, he noticed the McWilliamses' boys had once again been playing with scissors. He chuckled out loud when the boys' mother, Ann, caught him grinning at them, and she raised her hands as if signaling she had given up on those two ever having a decent haircut again. He was thankful to see B.C. Lee and his wife, Cindy, had returned safely from their vacation to the mountains. Mrs. Boleware was busy keeping her three little girls from talking.

He noticed Angela Thompson, a country doctor from a neighboring town, was down visiting her mother again. His mind wandered back to when she was just a little girl who loved to hunt and fish and, quite frankly, was a better shot than all the boys and half the grown men in the county.

He chuckled again as he remembered a Wednesday night service right before the beginning of deer season. Little Angie, as he called her back then, donned in her pink dress with blond ponytail, asked to lead the closing prayer: "Dear Lord, you know deer season is this Saturday, and I want to pray for all the hunters. And, Lord, you know that big buck is mine and don't let Pete or Timmy get it, especially Timmy. Amen."

Little Timmy was making a beeline to the front of the church to speak to God as well when his daddy grabbed him by the belt loop and hurried him out the door. Those two young'uns didn't stop their fierce competition until they got married years later.

As Brother Johnson continued to scan the room, he noticed a young man who appeared most uncomfortable, sitting on the back row. He watched as the man nervously looked around the room. Soon, one of the Boleware girls noticed the stranger and greeted him by sticking her tongue out toward him. The stranger returned the greeting causing the preacher to laugh.

The New Job 8

The alarm clock sounded off at 5:30 a.m. Up until this moment, he had tolerated his new challenge. Sure, he fretted with each new event that came his way. The dilapidated home, the daily injuries, the sweaty work crews telling him what to do, the lack of cigarettes and alcohol, the summer temperatures, the country foods, the lack of nightlife in this small town, and even the uncomfortable worship services were all bearable because he knew the end reward. However, getting up before the sun rose was more than he could tolerate. Thanks to Eleanor, Jon would be the newest employee at McElhaney's Feed and Seed, the local farm supply store. The hours of torture, as Jon put it, were between six-thirty and three o'clock.

He rolled over, slowly draping his feet over the side of the bed. He hated his feet touching the bare floor. Jon had already used all the money allotted for repairs in his new home. Eleanor would not allow him to call his father for extra money needed for paint and flooring. The truth was Eleanor did not have a clue where his father was. It was part of the agreement: no contact. There had been a contact number set up with his father's attorney, reserved for emergencies only, and as far as Eleanor was concerned, flooring and paint did not qualify as an emergency. He would have to purchase this on his own. He hated Eleanor today more than any other time. In fact, he hated life in general. The days had begun to run together. He was not sure if it was day thirty, thirty-one, or thirty-two.

$$$

Billy Wade Thompson, a very likable but sorely uneducated man, had been working at McElhaney's ever since dropping out of high school in the tenth grade at the age of eighteen. Growing up on a farm since birth, he knew all about farming supplies, frontward and backward, but he lacked the education to run the business end of the store. For this very reason, he would remain assistant storeroom helper until he retired. Sadly, he would probably be working until the day he died. It did not take Jon long to figure out Billy Wade was dumb as a rock—something everyone knew—but Billy Wade's six-foot-six statue prevented them from saying something about it.

Until Jon could save enough money for a vehicle, he would rely on Henry for a ride to town each morning.

"Good luck, son." Henry tried to cheer up the young man. The trip into town was dead quiet. Jon was not a morning person, and it showed.

As he stood on the front porch of the store, staring at all the metal pieces farmers used, he just shook his head. He did not know why Eleanor would pick something so obviously wrong for him. Soon, the McElhaney's employees arrived. Janice, the only one with a key, was in charge of accounting. The brothers Freddie and Wilton were mechanics; neither had an education past grade school, but they could fix anything on wheels. Dragging in last was Pete. He was the only one who went on to college, majoring in agriculture. His office was in the back. He also would, from time to time, work the counter if Billy Wade was gone. Pete and his older brother, James, owned the store. James McElhaney always arrived later in the day. Usually, his four-hundred-acre farm kept him too busy to come to the store every day.

"You must be the new guy?" Janice said as she unlocked the door.

Soon, the lights were on and the coffee pot steaming with fresh coffee. The men stood around waiting for the pot to stop dripping. Janice handed him his apron and name tag.

"Excuse me?" Jon said in disbelief.

"Something wrong, son?" Pete inquired in his slow country draw.

"What's with this?" Jon showed everyone the name tag.

Everyone giggled just a little.

"I believe that there might be an abbreviation."

"What idiot abbreviates Jonathan with Jonat?"

"I think Billy Wade was having a little trouble trying to fit your entire name on the badge."

"I'm not wearing this," he stated and threw it back on the counter.

"Well, we'll get you a new one as soon as the machine gets back from Hattiesburg. Billy Wade broke the dang thing yesterday."

In walked the homegrown countryman, saying, "You must be the new guy?"

Billy Wade nearly knocked the newest employee over with a big pat on the back. He had to be the biggest person that Jon had ever seen.

"Janice!" he hollered toward the back room. "Where's that name tag I made this feller?"

Pete and Wilton walked by and patted the new employee on the shoulder, as Billy Wade pinned the badge on the apron.

"Looks like you're all set." Jon looked at the others for a little help, but Pete just winked at the sight of the name tag pinned to Jon's shirt, and Wilton had to turn his head for fear of laughing too loud.

After about four hours of trying to explain his name to everyone he helped, he gave up. Between Billy Wade, screaming his new nickname on the intercom all day, and the little woman, who told her husband that Jonat was probably French, Jon decided then and there to never set foot back in the south again after this year was all over.

At eleven sharp, all the employees, except Janice, walked down the street to the little diner for lunch. Jon was still angry at his new nightmare of a job and just grabbed a bag of chips as he walked outside. The big town of Red Clay consisted of the farm supply store, the café, a beauty shop, two churches, Doc's office—which still looked like a home with the big porch draped across the front—Janson's Pharmacy, a gas station/barber shop, and the new video store, which was at the moment the talk of the town. And of course, there was the vegetable stand set up at the corner of Main and Central.

At two o'clock sharp, the delivery truck from the coast arrived. Billy Wade had a system set up for deliveries. When the delivery bell rang, everyone but Janice proceeded to the warehouse-receiving door. Someone would climb onto the truck and start throwing the bags of whatever was being delivered to the next one in line. Soon, all the bags would be tossed to the back of the warehouse. Jon went to see where everyone had gone and unintentionally stepped into the tossing line. The last thing Jon remembered were the words: "Hey, Jonat, catch."

The fifty-pound bag of fertilizer, along with Billy Wade's tossing strength, proved to be too much for the slender-built young man—Jon—with his arms wrapped around the bag was flung through the doorway and into the store. He slid on his back across the floor, landing at the feet of Sam Rogers.

"You must be the Frenchman I've been hearing about. I'd get that stuff off your face. You know that's fertilizer, don't you?" Sam laughed until he fell backward into a potting soil display.

Sam was Evie's youngest son and had just arrived home from college.

$$$

"Momma, it's just a scratch." Sam hated being babied, especially in front of the man he had just spent twenty minutes laughing at.

"Hold still, Sammy," Evie protested, using his childhood name.

"Yeah, hold still, Sammy-boy. We wouldn't want that dangerous Band-Aid to slip or something," Jon joked, happy to finally be able to ridicule someone else for a change.

Evie turned her head toward the man covered in fertilizer. "You're next, Jonat."

Jon's bump on his head turned out to be okay, but because he was a tad bit stinky, his boss gave him the rest of the day off. He was grateful to Sam for the ride home. The boys seemed to hit it off. Each one was taking shots at the other.

"So, Jonat, you been in this country long?" Sam started.

"Ha! Ha! Very funny, Sammy-boy. Have you ever met anyone as dumb as Billy Wade?"

"Don't call me that!" referring to the nickname, *Sammy-boy*. "Hey, you want to go fishing?" Sam noticed the pond as the two passed the forty acres.

"In this heat?" Jon stayed as close to the air-conditioning as possible.

"Oh, come on. It'll be fun. That pond is loaded with fish. The old man who lived here wouldn't let us fish, so we used to sneak down here when he wasn't looking." He jumped out of the truck and retrieved the fishing poles stored in the back. "I don't go anywhere without these things. Years ago, there was this monster fish we all called Bub. We all hooked him at least once, but no one could ever get him to the bank." He paused, looking around at the farm. "You've done some work here. I don't understand why a city boy like you wanted to live here." He gave Jon one of the poles and then headed down to the barn.

Jon followed, asking, "What are you looking for?"

Sam explained that there used to be a Catawba worm tree or a worm bed next to the barn. He could not quite remember which. Jon walked cautiously through the barn. Sam seemed to fear nothing as he went inside the chicken coop.

"Hey, look at all these eggs. Why don't you get them?" Sam noticed Jon's uneasiness around the chickens. "Help me get them. You could sell them at McElhaney's."

Jon explained about the mites and the rooster that attacked him.

"You mean that rooster?" Sam pointed to the fact that the satanic rooster in question had escaped the chicken coop again and was coming up behind him.

Sam took pure joy in watching Jon dance around the rooster's constant strikes. Soon, eggs were flying everywhere as Sam attempted to scare the rooster away. Before long, both Jon and the rooster were covered with raw eggs. The rooster retreated, leaving Jon trying to catch his breath. "I hate that thing."

Sam, on the other hand, was rolling on the ground in pain from laughing so hard. "Why don't you just shoot it?"

The look on Jon's face was priceless. Once again, the carpenters had played another joke on him.

"You mean to tell me it is not illegal to kill them?"

"They make good eating. That's what I'd do." They both walked cautiously around the edge of the barn.

"I've never seen a rooster so mean, and I grew up with raising them."

The two of them, mostly Sam, caught fish until dark and stopped only for a bite of Esther's supper. Eleanor was glad to see the young man having fun for the first time since arriving. Sam shared his dreams of owning his own farm and planting pecan trees. He had planned every detail of his future life, including his wife.

"I plan on marrying Caroline as soon as she gets through with school."

"Caroline from Doc Rogers's office?"

"Yep. But don't tell anyone."

"Why?"

"Just because."

"Why not?"

"Caroline Thompson. Need I say more?"

"Thompson?" He thought for a minute, and then it clicked. "Oh, man! Are you crazy? Do you actually want those genes in your family tree?"

With that remark, Sam pushed Jon into the water.

Sam could see his mother's van coming down the road. "Well, the fun's over. Here comes Momma."

The two boys walked up the hill to the sound of Evie blowing the horn.

"Good Lord, son. You had me worried sick!"

"Is she always this protective of her Sammy-boy?" Jon joked.

"More so, since the cancer has come back."

"Cancer? She got cancer?"

"Nope. I do. Want to go mud riding down by the river tomorrow?"

"Okay." Jon could not believe the news. Sam was so lively and fun. Until now, he could not recall knowing anyone who had cancer.

"I'll pick you up from work. Then afterward, we can take care of that little problem down by the barn."

Jon sat on the porch, looking at the stars. He had never known anyone like Sam before.

Boys Will Be Boys　　　9

Although Evie worried a great deal about her son, she knew it was best to let him live life to the fullest. Sam had always been one to enjoy whatever came his way. Two years earlier, when he was first diagnosed with cancer, Sam took on the challenge full force. No one ever heard him complain when the chemo began to get the better of him, but his mother knew. Mothers always know. Evie was relieved when the cancer went into remission. Sam was the strong one when the doctor reported that the cancer had resurfaced.

Each day, Evie was thankful for the smiles and funny tales that Sam brought home, whether it was Sam laughing at Jon trying to wring the rooster's neck, or Jon trying his best not to laugh in the face of Billy Wade, while Sam stood off hidden in the distance making faces. The boys had something to tell every day.

Her favorite to date was how Sam tricked Jon into the choir loft during morning service about two weeks earlier. Evie laughed all through the service as Jon sat nauseously in the choir. Jon tried his best to get the words out of his mouth. Sam, on the other hand, could not carry a tune, but that did not stop him from making a joyful noise. Adding to the comedy was the fact the minister of music asked them both not to come back. The entire service was riddled with laughter as the two young men tried their best to add to the all-women's choir.

Sam's singing loud and Jon's singing of the wrong verses were even more than Pastor Johnson could handle as he stepped up to the pulpit.

"Well, how about that!" the preacher asked.

The congregation could no longer hold their laughter, which made matters worse for even this seasoned pastor. The minister of music, Dee Brady, was embarrassed with everyone laughing. Stella and her twin sister, Della Anderson, both retired schoolteachers and lifelong choir members, had never remembered a time when the all-women's choir had sounded so awful. The two unmarried women had enough and departed the choir loft as fast as two eighty-two-year-olds could go. When Della swung her purse at the grinning boys, accidentally knocking out Stella's false teeth into Pearlee McIntyre's lap, Pastor Johnson put his head down on the wooden podium and whispered, "Lord Jesus, take me now!"

It took the pastor many days and several trips to the old women's home before both agreed to return to the church, let alone sing in the choir again.

The pastor called the boys into his office after Wednesday night prayer meeting. In addition, Evie made the boys go and apologize to all the women. Someone even suggested to the deacons that maybe the boys would like to clean up around the church in an effort to make amends. Jon thought this was ridiculous. Sam suggested they should attend the new holistic church that recently came to town. Jon agreed because he had no intention of cleaning the church.

$$$

When the next Sunday came around, Jon headed to the make-shift double-wide church. He was standing outside when the pastor approached him.

"Are you Jon?" he asked.

"I am."

"Sam called. He will be a few minutes late. Come on in, and we'll get started."

As best that Jon could tell, the congregation consisted of the pastor, his wife, four children, an infant, and two men. The two men Jon believed the law could very well have wanted them both. Jon began to get worried when Sam did not show up. The singing was over, and the two men carried a wooden box, placing it in front of the small congregation. Soon, everyone joined hands and encircled the pastor. Jon watched nervously as the two men opened the mysterious box. Although new at this church business, he felt sure this was not a Baptist thing. And he was right.

As Jon bolted through the front doors, he found Sam had been waiting, sitting on the hood of Henry's truck holding a camera in hand. Jon stumbled to the truck. The only thing Jon hated more than roosters was snakes, and when the pastor began to pass the slivering serpents around, he knew his afternoon would be spent cleaning up the First Baptist Church of Red Clay, Mississippi.

"I'll get you! I'll get you!" he shouted, backing the truck away from the snake-infested church. "I'll get you," he shouted again out the window.

Jon had every intention of spilling the beans about Sam and Billy Wade's precious only daughter, Caroline, just as soon as McElhaney's opened up the next morning.

Sandy   10

"Eight years old," Della and Stella said practically at the same time, expressing their disbelief that a parent did not accompany the little boy. On Wednesday nights, for as long as anyone could remember, the women were in charge of helping with the evening meal. Once, the sisters were in charge of many tasks at First Baptist Church of Red Clay, Mississippi. But now due to their age, they were reduced to being dessert servers and choir members.

When the younger generation insisted the women give up their church duties, Della exclaimed loudly, "Over my dead body." The thought sent Stella into the hospital with a case of the nerves. The younger generation had forgotten that the Anderson sisters had furnished the entire kitchen many, many years ago. It was not until Della had the deacons remove everything but the kitchen sink and put it on their front porch did the congregation realize how important serving the Lord meant to these two founding members. The pastor spent many sleepless nights trying to create a compromise. Weeks passed before the stubborn women agreed to re-donate the kitchen, and the deacons spent many hours putting everything back to the way it was. By that time, everyone was tired of having sandwiches for Wednesday night supper. Finally, everyone agreed, but the younger women still griped about the oversized servings of dessert the sisters were dishing out, but no one on the meal committee dared to say anything to them.

The young visitor sat quietly by himself, eating his meal as if he had not eaten in a week. Little did they know how close to the truth it was. The children's group leader invited the youngster to join the activities, but he declined. Della thought that maybe it was because the child feared the other youngsters would ridicule him. Stella insisted that the deacons get the key to open the clothes' closet. The two women sorted through the boxes, finding shirts and pants that would surely fit the child. The women vowed he would be properly dressed. They also boxed the remaining cookies from supper so that the child could take them home.

Jon and Sam had taken their usual seats on the back row. Ever since Billy Wade mysteriously found out about Sam and his daughter, the lovebirds did not have to sneak around anymore. Although by now Jon was accustomed to the routine of church, he was glad to have his new friend by his side, even if it meant sharing the overly crowded back row with Billy Wade, his wife, Nettie, and Sam's girlfriend. Just as the announcements were beginning, the eight-year-old squeezed into the back pew. It did not take Jon long to realize the child needed a bath.

"Hey, I'm Sandy," the young man whispered and extended his hand.

"Well, Sandy, do you think you could be still?" Jon whispered back, wiping something greasy off his hands.

"I'll try, but my head itches."

"Want some gum?" Jon asked.

The child's breath smelled horrible.

After that, Sandy followed Jon around like glue. When the service was over, the women gave the child the clothes and the cookies. Della insisted someone give the little visitor a ride home. Henry had already left with Eleanor. Sam was going to the movies with Caroline. Two of the deacons and their wives were still cleaning the fellowship hall, and the other one was giving the Anderson sisters a ride home. The pastor needed to get to the hospital, and the children's director was waiting on late parents. It was going to be either Jon or Evie and the doctor. As Jon's luck would have it, the doctor received a call from the emergency room. Evie laughed as the two climbed into Jon's newly purchased Chevy S-10.

"How come you got a really old truck?" The endless supply of questions began.

"It's not that old."

"How come it looks so old?"

"It's not that old."

"But how come it looks so old?"

"It's not old!" Jon raised his voice as politely as he could without scaring the kid.

"But it looks old."

"Okay! It's old." Jon gave up.

"Does the radio work?"

"No."

"How come?"

"I don't know."

"It's probably because it is old."

"Where are those patches?" Jon regretted he had stopped using the nicotine patches.

"What patches?" the curious child asked.

"Never mind," Jon answered.

"You married?" the child continued.

"No. And stop scratching your head."

"How come?"

"How come what? To stop scratching?" Jon was confused.

"No, how come you not married?"

"None of your business."

Jon hoped that would stop the questions, but it did not.

They continued until they reached the child's house.

"Turn here," instructed Sandy.

"Why is it dark in your house? Where are your parents?" Jon found himself concerned for the first time about the boy.

"My dad's gone somewhere. I don't know." Sandy climbed out of the truck. "Thanks for the ride and the gum," he continued.

The boxes were too bulky for the small child to handle by himself, and Jon was needed to tote them inside.

"Turn the lights on. I can't see where I'm going," Jon said with irritation in his voice as he had tripped upon entering the home.

"They don't work."

"What do you mean they don't work?"

"Sometimes, they work, sometimes, they don't." It was a normal event for this child.

Jon went to the truck and retrieved his flashlight. Something was not right. Jon did not know it at the time, but this night would change his life forever.

"Where's your mother?"

This time, it was Jon asking all the questions.

"She went to the store." It was the truth as the child knew it.

"When did she go?" Jon saw the kitchen counter littered with open jars and cookies, a carton of milk left out on the counter had curdled.

"I think last Tuesday. I don't remember. She will be back. She always comes back."

Eleanor's lights in the RV were already out when he had come home last night. When Jon's alarm clock sounded, he wasted no time in waking the child. He knew Eleanor would have all the answers.

$$$

The sheriff's office placed a missing report on Sandy's mother, but no one had any hope of finding the addict. According to Sheriff Steele, Sandra Henderson had a rap sheet as tall as Sandy, mostly with shoplifting and drug charges. Little Sandy had been placed in foster care five times already, and he refused to go there again.

Eleanor suggested to the sheriff, "Why don't you let us keep the lad?"

"What?" Jon disagreed. "No!"

"Esther and I can watch the boy until you get home from work, and then you can take care of him."

It was official, Eleanor surely had lost her mind. Unfortunately for Jon, everyone thought the idea was great. Jon headed to his truck, followed closely by one happy little boy, asking, "You got anymore gum?"

$$$

Over the course of the next few days, Jon's world changed again. Sam began chemo treatments, and Evie would not allow visitors. At the store, Jon stayed more confused than helpful. He was learning, but it was slow. Some of the employees gave him a hard time.

Pete said, "I reckon if Billy Wade could learn it. It can be learned."

Making matters worse was the fact that Sandy's head itching turned out to be head lice. Both he and Jon now sported crew cuts, compliments of Henry. Since staying at the farm, the lad had gained eight pounds.

"I'm hungry," Sandy declared.

"You're always hungry."

"But I really am," he protested.

The boys had been painting the living room. Jon had finally been able to purchase paint, and both were covered head to toe with specks of sage green.

"All right. Let's go."

They were off to Bea's Diner for a burger. Although Sandy enjoyed Esther's home cooking, he was quite fond of cheeseburgers. On weekends, Esther and Henry were always gone, and Eleanor preferred to relax.

Bea's was the only diner in the small town, and everyone loved her cooking. Sometimes after Sunday worship, Jon's new family would head to Lee Springs, a town twenty-five miles to the south for one of the many nicer restaurants.

But on Saturdays, Bea's was all there was.

The diner reeked country with its red-checkered tablecloths and mason-jar tea glasses. Each table was decorated with a single pink flower, sitting high out of an old-fashioned Coke bottle. The waitresses knew everyone by name, including Jon and Sandy. Miss Bea, owner and operator, baked biscuits from scratch every morning, and the hamburgers were homemade from the charcoal grill, not pre-cut frozen patties cooked in a frying pan. For fifty-five cents more, homemade chili would add extra flavor to any burger. In addition to the homemade biscuits, Bea made pies and cakes. Jon and Sandy both favored the triple layer chocolate cake.

"Come on in, boys." Bea looked up from behind the glass dessert counter when the cowbell jiggled, signaling the door opening. "I just frosted a chocolate cake. Figured y'all be in soon," she continued.

"Cheeseburger, Miss Bea!" Sandy shouted his order across the room.

"Make mine a double with chili!" followed Jon.

Usually by one-thirty, the lunch crowd thinned to nothing. The few waitresses Bea trusted to uphold the reputation of her establishment had waned down to two—one to serve, and the other to replenish the tables after the hungry lunch crowd left. Occasionally, Bea would get out-of-town folk who dropped by for directions or coffee. When the cowbell jingled, Jon and Sandy turned to see who had come in. Bea hurried to greet her guest.

"Come in, sit anywhere you like."

"Gross, we're not eating here, Daddy," informed the oldest of the three girls.

Alvin Young peeped his head through the serving window. Big Al had been cooking for Bea since she opened in the '80s.

"Hush," the father quickly instructed the twenty-year-old.

Sandy giggled.

"Steven, don't embarrass her in front of these people," his wife scolded.

"Who's she calling 'these people?'" Jon spoke loudly enough for everyone to hear.

"I'm sorry. It's been a long ride, and I think we're all a little tired," the man spoke.

He was trying to smooth things over with Bea the best he could.

"It's all right, honey. What can I do for you?"

"I'm Dr. Steve Garvin from Jackson, and I am supposed to meet with Dr. and Mrs. Rogers this afternoon, but I'm afraid I might be a little lost."

"Oh, I believe you missed that last right turn about a mile back. You can't miss it. Just turn by that big red barn."

"Thanks."

Since he had forgotten to stop by the bakery and get the cake his wife had ordered, he suggested taking one of Bea's cakes to the Roger's home.

"Monica, what about one of those?" He pointed to the display case.

"We have coconut, apple, lemon, strawberry, and chocolate." Bea was proud of her blue ribbon cake recipes. "Can I cut you a piece?" she continued.

"How much for the whole cake?" the man asked.

"Thirty dollars plus tax." Bea was excited about the sale.

"Which one?" the mother asked the girls.

"Not the chocolate one," shouted Sandy from the booth, as he had been eavesdropping on their conversation.

The girls looked over in Sandy's direction and wrinkled their noses at the dirty country boys. "We want the chocolate one, Daddy," they spoke in unison.

"No!" Sandy protested again.

"Chocolate it is," said the mother.

"I think those boys had their eyes on that one, dear," the husband said, once again embarrassed by the girls.

"Steven, just pay her. You drag us out to this, this, whatever you call this place. We'll be in the car."

Monica Garvin usually made his life miserable. She and the girls wanted no part in his dream of moving to the country—a decision he made after the local police department charged their oldest child, Stephanie, with possession of controlled substance. The middle child, eighteen-year-old Elisabeth, seemed to be following along her sister's footsteps, with curfew violations and a recent DUI. The girls' legal troubles had already cost the father big bucks and several favors from high-ranking officials. The littlest Garvin, Anna, was the apple of her father's eye, and he intended to keep her that way. The country life meant giving up his six-figure income, but he had had enough. Then there was the issue of his wife; he was not able to prove it, but he had suspicions his wife was having an affair with his partner.

Bea hated more than anything to sell the whole cake, but she had no choice. She placed the cake inside the white cardboard box and totaled the register.

"That will be thirty-two dollars and ten cents," she informed the father.

"How about doing me a small favor first?" the out-of-town visitor asked Bea.

And to Bea's delight, she did just that.

Bea sliced two pieces of the chocolate cake, and the doctor carried the plates over to the table. Sandy had already put his head down on the table, pouting.

"Are you the young fellow who ordered chocolate cake?"

The pouting child raised his head from the table. The teardrops slowly falling down his face, coupled with the few small puddles on the table, were evidence the lad had had his heart set on the cake especially made for him. At least Bea always made him feel like she baked it just for him. Many times in his life, his heart had been broken, but now thanks to this community, he was feeling loved—real love—for the first time. In addition, Jon too was learning about true love, only he did not recognize it just yet.

Sandy raised his head and wiped his face with his shirttail. Jon rolled his eyes at the table manners and tossed him a balled up napkin, hitting him in the forehead that made everyone laugh.

Farmers by Two   11

Days turned into weeks, and before long, the two boys stuck together like glue. Jon even failed to notice his long journey was more than one-third over. The locals were considering him as one of the regular town folk by now. The Anderson sisters were no longer mad at him and even used his help from time to time. Jon turned the egg business over to Sandy to give the boy spending money. At least, that is what Jon was telling everyone. But truth be known, the chickens still scared the daylights out of him. Sam was enduring his treatment well and tolerating his mother only fairly. It had been weeks since the young man had been over to the farm. The Garvins were settling into the community. Everyone was pleased to have two doctors in such a small town. Monica still spent her days in either New Orleans or Jackson, sometimes staying overnight. The girls hated the country life and filled their days breaking the speed limits on the gravel roads and talking on the phone to friends back home. Both could not wait until the fall semester. Stephanie was returning as a junior, although barely passing, and Elisabeth was ready for life as a freshman. Frankly, the townspeople thought little of his wife and the oldest two girls, but all who met him liked the doctor. Little Anna found true love in none other than Sandy. Sandy's mother was still a no-show.

Jon learned many lessons pertaining to cattle farming. The men at McElhaney's gathered around the coffee pot each morning, enjoying Henry's tales about Jon and Sandy and whatever livestock that was giving them trouble the previous day. After four hours stuck in the top of an oak tree, Jon and Sandy both understood the importance of closing the gates behind them. Luckily, the mail carrier heard them yelling and summoned B.C. Lee and his boys from the farm two miles down the road to get the bull out of the pasture. The next Saturday, Jon sold the twelve-hundred-pound Brahman bull at the stockyard.

Everyone's favorite story to date was when someone at the feed store gave Sandy a rope. The lad roped everything in sight until the day he actually lassoed a cow. He was so proud of his catch that he tied his end of the rope to the truck to show Jon. Sandy was standing in the bed of the truck, yelling at the top of his lungs trying to get Jon's attention. Before Jon noticed, the cow realized she was unable to leave and began to jump and kick to high heaven. Sandy leaped from the truck and ran all the way home, leaving the truck to the mercy of the angry momma cow, who wanted nothing more than to get away. Jon's old truck was beat up one side and down the other before Jon realized what was going on. Jon had to call upon B.C. Lee once again.

"They don't like to be tied up, son," B.C. Lee stated in his slow country accent, as he and his boys watched in disbelief at the angry cow.

"You think?" Jon was embarrassed and aggravated at the same time.

"I don't reckon I know what to do right off the bat. Give me a minute to think." The farmer scratched his head and then continued, "I guess I've never seen this before."

Jon wanted to drag the words out of his mouth faster. After all, his truck was losing the battle. "Well, can you think any faster?"

"Well," B.C. continued.

"Well, what?" Jon threw up his hands. "Hurry! While there is something still left of my truck."

"I reckon we just got to let her tire herself out."

"What?" he shouted in disbelief.

"Yep, I reckon that's what will do it."

And it did. Before long, the cow stopped, and B.C. walked over and released the lasso from around her horns. Surprisingly, the truck cranked. When Jon finally made it to the house, Sandy was nowhere to be found. On the counter was a handwritten apology and twenty-four dollars and seventeen cents—Sandy's egg money from the previous three weeks. Jon called out for the boy, but Sandy stayed hidden under the bed for fear of foster care. Jon stood at the kitchen window, drinking a glass of cold water when, unexpectedly, a forgotten memory from his past emerged. Jon began to laugh uncontrollably when he remembered he had done the same thing to his own father. Only it was not an old truck, but rather his father's new Mercedes that he and a few friends had taken for a spin around the country club when he was twelve.

Sandy listened carefully from the safety of his room, as Jon yelled, "I'm going to Bea's for a burger. You better come on if you're hungry."

Sandy heard the front door open and close. Seconds after, when the truck cranked, he darted at full speed out the door, grabbing the money off the counter and leaping into the back of the truck. Eleanor and Esther, returning from the grocery store, watched as the child waved as the truck passed by her RV.

Eleanor asked Henry's wife, "What do you suppose happened to that truck?"

Sandy stood with arms extended wide open, grinning from ear to ear as the wind whipped around his body. Jon's flashback from the past warmed his heart with joy. It was his grandfather's recollection that kept him from getting into trouble for wrecking the car. He said Jon's father had done the same thing when he was young. It was good to remember his grandfather's laughter.

$$$

Bea had just put a fresh cake into the glassed cooler box when the cowbell jingled.

"Hey, Miss Bea!" he yelled across the counter then jumped and spun around on one of the barstools. "I'm hungry."

Barbara Perkins, Bea's oldest waitress, walked by the boy, spinning him once more, and said, "What's new about that?"

Jon took the stool next to Sandy in order to stop the child's spinning.

"What'll it be today, boys?"

In the eyes of Sandy, Barbara Perkins had to be the oldest person he knew, even older than the Anderson sisters. The truth was she was younger than Bea, but her life had been hard. Thanks to the tips she made at this job, she was able to leave her abusive husband for good. She met Bea in a crowded waiting room in Hattiesburg while both were waiting to see the orthopedic doctor. Bea was returning for a recheck on a sprained ankle, and Barbara had endured another night of torment at the hands of her drunken husband. Bea, like Eleanor, had a way of understanding what others in need were feeling. At first, Barbara was withdrawn, but Bea had a special way about her, and before long, she offered to help the teary-eyed woman. Barbara walked out of that clinic with Bea and into a new life. Barbara still laughs about how the two of them met and especially how she left her husband in the car, drinking a six-pack in the parking lot, unaware of her new plans. The first time Sandy ate at the diner, he asked Barbara, "How old are you?" Her response that time—and every time since then—always made the boy laugh.

"Hey, Barbara, how old are you today?" He spun the stool around again.

"Older than dirt, boy, older than dirt!" This was today's response, as she shouted from across the room, and everyone giggled.

The boys ate while the jukebox played the country tunes hand chosen by Sandy. He loved country music; Jon did not. Sandy would sing to anyone who would listen. Sometimes, the waitresses would join in. The cowbell jingled, and in walked Sandy's nightmare.

"Hey, Sandy," said the sweet little voice of Anna Garvin as she chose the barstool next to him.

Something about the little girl caused Sandy to lose his speech. No matter how much Jon picked at him, the child refused to talk in front of her.

Jon leaned forward to speak to the child. "Hello to little Cinderella and her wicked stepsisters."

He always made it a point to take a jab at Stephanie and Elisabeth, and they always replied back, "Country trash."

Anna's attention turned back to Sandy, "What happened to your truck, Sandy?"

The child continued to eat, pretending not to be able to talk while food was in his mouth.

Jon answered instead, "We had a little accident, didn't we, Sandy?"

Sandy shook his head at Jon, pleading with him not to tell what he had done.

The girls took the opportunity to jab back. "Is that what happened to your hair?"

Barbara could not help but to laugh at the comment. Their homemade crew cuts had been a sight for some time now.

It was at this time that Sandy chose to stand up and be a man, so to speak. He shouted back to the giggling girls, "This is not our real haircuts. We had lice! So there!"

Barbara burst out laughing. Bea could no longer hold back the giggles and left the counter. Jon was now speechless at Sandy's attempt to tell the girls off.

Stephanie yelled, "Gross. Anna, get away. They have bugs."

Elisabeth picked her little sister off the barstool and left the restaurant.

Jon sat motionless, looking at Sandy eating the last bite of his burger. He yelled, "Get in the truck."

Through the kitchen-serving window, everyone could hear Big Al rolling with laughter.

$$$

The sheriff was waiting on the porch when the boys returned home from lunch. Henry said there was no easy way to deliver bad news except to just say it. Other than his grandfather's death, Jon never had to deal with this kind of situation. His grandfather's health had deteriorated badly before finally falling into a coma three weeks before passing on. Although Jon was young at the time, he witnessed firsthand how his grandfather suffered and was actually relieved once he passed. But this death was unexpected, and Jon struggled to come to terms how God could take someone so young. Eleanor thought it was best if she broke the news to Sandy.

Unseen Blessing 12

Evie insisted on being completely in charge of the funeral arrangements. She and the doctor made sure the young man was treated as if he were family, even buying him a new suit and dress shoes. The service, held at Johnson's Funeral Home, would be at ten o'clock in the morning. The Anderson sisters would open their home to friends and family after the graveside service was over. Pearlee McIntyre would be bringing her much-talked-about chicken and dumplings. Mrs. Bea made two chocolate cakes. Billy Wade Thompson fried a turkey, and the McElhaney boys smoked a ham. Food had been arriving all morning. Esther and a few women from the church would stay at the Anderson's in order to have the food ready to serve following the funeral.

Jon and Eleanor sat on the front pew next to him. The deacons of First Baptist Church of Red Clay served as pallbearers, and the ladies' choir sang the young man's favorite hymns. Jon was trying to be strong, but he could not hold back the tears. Everyone was saddened. One by one, everyone made his or her way by the casket. All spoke words like, "So young, and it's such a shame." Sandy sat quietly between Jon and Eleanor. This was the first funeral he had ever been to, and he was too scared to move. Everyone listened attentively to Pastor Johnson's beautiful description of how Heaven would be.

When the funeral home director asked everyone to rise as the casket began to leave the building, Sandy walked over to his mother, laid his head down on her beautiful oak casket, and wrapped his little arms around her as best he could. Eleanor closed her eyes in

65

silent prayer, asking for strength and comfort for the child. Jon, with overflowing tears, walked over and bent down on his knees. Another memory surfaced from Jon's past, this time of his grandfather's funeral. Jon placed his arms around the brokenhearted child and whispered into his ears, "Your mother needs"—he paused, for the words were too hard—"she needs to go, Sandy."

The child let go, and he held tightly around Jon's neck. Not one person in the room had dry eyes. Jon had managed to get the words out. This was the hardest thing he had ever done and now knew how his father had felt when he said the same thing to him years ago.

The child kissed the casket once more, saying, "Goodbye, Mommy."

Eleanor thought it best not to tell Sandy his mother had died of a drug overdose. Authorities were still trying to locate the boy's father, and Sandy could not remember if he still had grandparents or not. For now, it was best if the boy stayed where he was. The sheriff agreed.

The Baptists, known for providing food in times of need, had certainly provided. The Anderson's home filled with people who had adopted the child into their hearts. Even the Garvin girls showed they actually had hearts. Over the next few weeks, Sandy clung to Eleanor. Jon found himself actually missing the child, especially when time came to collect the eggs each day. Soon, school would be starting, and she hoped that would help distract the child from his sadness.

$$$

News was out that Sam had purchased the forty acres down the road from Eleanor's RV. Against the advice of Evie, he wanted to start clearing the land in time to plant the pecan trees in January. Sam had talked his father into investing, so to speak, in his dream. Jon could not wait until they were neighbors and especially could not wait until Sam was cancer-free again. When the chemo took Sam's hair, Jon shaved his head too. Everyone agreed the baldhead was better than the lopsided crew cut he had been sporting for weeks. Sandy decided not to take part in the head shaving due to school starting and all. Jon believed the "and all" meant Anna Garvin.

If Jon's best friend was not at the doctor's office or Caroline's house, he was thumbing through the fruit tree catalogs at the farm store. He wanted to be completely sure he chose the best ones before he ordered the trees.

"You made your mind up, son?" Pete asked Sam. "You know you should order those things before the middle of September, don't you?"

Sam sat on the counter as he always did, watching out for Billy Wade to return. "Almost, Pete, almost. I've got it down to two."

Things between Sam and Caroline were going at full speed. No matter how much her daddy protested, she refused to finish junior college. Billy Wade knew firsthand how important book learning was, but she wanted only to be married to Sam Rogers. Besides, they did not know exactly how much time on this earth he had left. Chemo was almost over, and that was just one of the coming celebrations. Caroline was pregnant, almost four months, and soon, everyone would know. She would wait to tell Sam when his last chemo treatment was over, two weeks away. She did not want anything to interfere with his recovery. Although Evie already had her suspicions about the so-called stomach flu the young woman could not get over, she remained silent on the issue. Evie worried more about Billy Wade Thompson, knowing his precious baby girl would soon be a mother herself, than she did about the secret pregnancy.

Before September was over, Sam had the pecan trees ordered and a ring on his now-fiancé's hand. Of course, it took Evie swinging a baseball bat over Billy Wade's head to convince him to release the grip he had on her son.

"Let go of him right now, you big ox! I swear, I'm fixing to take you out of this world, Billy Wade, if you don't put my son down right now."

The doc put four stitches—free of charge, of course—into the thickheaded man. A few weeks would pass by before the new grandfather-to-be finally accepted the fact his world was changing and there would be nothing he could do to change it back. Soon, his focus shifted to the fact a grandchild was arriving, and he and the doc went in together to put a mobile home on Sam's forty acres.

$$$

Two months into the new school year, Sandy decided he would return to Jon's house. Eleanor had done a good job getting him into a daily routine, and the child had bounced back from the loss of his mother better than everyone had hoped. Each school morning, Sam would drive Caroline to work and drop Sandy off to school because Jon still had to be at work at six-thirty. Then he would either travel to Hattiesburg for a checkup or work at the farm, preparing for the trees depending on his schedule.

By now, Jon's life had fallen into a routine. He could answer most questions regarding bugs, fertilizer, fruit trees, and many other things pertaining to the farm store. On Wednesdays, he had dinner at church, and thanks to Eleanor, he was in charge of making the coffee—a feat the church family endured until he learned. Eleanor said that each week, Sandy needed rewarding for the good grades he was making at school. So each Friday, the boys ate at Bea's, if his test grades were passing.

Sandy sat patiently, well as patiently as a young boy could, waiting for Jon to come home. Eleanor had already warned the child that Jon was working late, and they would probably have to postpone that Friday's trip to Bea's until the following day. The delivery truck had broken down somewhere between Jackson and Hattiesburg, causing McElhaney's employees to remain at the store until seven-thirty. Nevertheless, that did not matter to the child. In each hand was perfect scores: one in spelling and the other in math. He was sure Jon would not be too tired to celebrate those grades. But Eleanor had been right again. When Jon finally made it home, he was too tired to go out for dinner, falling asleep minutes after walking through the door.

By the time Saturday's suppertime came around, the boys were more than hungry. Half the day was spent putting up a fence at Sam's place, and the other half was spent chasing cows because someone left the gate open again. Jon had narrowed the suspects down to "not me" and "I don't know." He laughed out loud for he remembered those two shady characters vividly from his own childhood.

As he and Eleanor chased the remaining two cows back inside the fence, Jon laughed and said, "It's a wonder my father didn't give me away."

Eleanor replied, "What makes you think he didn't try?"

Jon laughed. Having Sandy around had been a blessing to Jon. He had begun to understand how hard it had been for his father. Jon knew he had been a difficult child.

"You are pretty good with these animals, you know," Eleanor said.

Jon looked around at the farm that finally felt like home and said, "Yeah. Maybe my father was right after all."

Eleanor just smiled.

Jon asked Sandy if he had gotten the eggs, and of course, he had not and took off like lightning, running to the barn. Jon propped his foot up on the barbed wire fence and listened to the calves mooing for their mommas. He now counted ten calves. Henry said that soon there would be more.

Jon waited in the truck while Sandy washed the chicken poop off his boots and off the floorboard.

"Okay, I'm ready!"

As always, he was hungry and talked about what he would order once there. If he was not talking, he was singing whatever tunes blared out the radio. Sometimes, Jon would join in just to make fun of the country song, but truth was, he was finally taking a liking to the music he once called prehistoric.

As they passed Sam's farm, Jon honked the horn.

"I think she is going to bust wide open." Sandy worried about Caroline's belly growing so big. "Have you ever seen one bust open?" he inquired.

Jon answered, shook his head no.

"Matt said his aunt in Georgia had a litter of babies." Jon laughed a little.

"Mrs. Holliman is going to have a baby real soon," Sandy declared.

Jon was not sure who that was.

"You know, my teacher. She's not as fat as Caroline," the young man explained.

"Do you think Sam's cancer is gone?" Sandy continued his non-stop questions.

Jon shrugged his shoulders.

"Hey! Did you see that deer?" Jon had already seen it and hit the brakes in an effort to avoid hitting it. "We are having a bake sale during recess next week." The endless talking continued.

Everyone could hear the two boys singing before they could see the truck, as they turned into the restaurant. Barbara, the waitress, had stepped outside to smoke a cigarette when they arrived.

"Hey, Barbara! How old are you?" Sandy shouted out the truck window.

Barbara thumped the butt on the ground, stepping on it to be sure it was out.

"Methuselah calls me Aunt Barbara, child." Sandy giggled.

"Your girlfriends are inside. And they brought company all the way from the big city itself," the waitress informed the two.

She made her already country voice even more country sounding to emphasize that the girls considered everyone in Red Clay as rednecks. The girls were the reason Barbara had borrowed a cigarette from a customer in the first place.

"Oh, this ought to be good. It's a shame my shift is almost over," Barbara said as she held the door open, as the boys walked through to watch the confrontation begin.

Stephanie whispered something the girls found amusing as the boys walked past them.

The boys were seated for quite some time when Sandy decided to rush things up.

"Hey, Barbara," Sandy hollered above the music coming from the jukebox, "how come you ain't took our order?"

The girls laughed out loud when Stephanie said, "See what I mean? 'Ain't.' The new waitress has you guys today. She'll be right with you."

Then Barbara shouted through the grill window, "Lily, you got customers."

"What new waitress?" Sandy asked, but Jon just shrugged his shoulders and continued looking at the menu. Sandy noticed her first. Instantly, he was in love with the brown-haired, blue-eyed waitress coming toward their table. "Hey, Jon, look at her."

As she walked past the table of spoiled rich girls, one of them used their foot to nonchalantly place a purse in the path of the unseasoned server. Sandy saw the entire episode, but Jon looked up just in time to receive the full force of the pitcher of water in his face, followed by the glasses, silverware, and—lastly—Lily herself. She was so embarrassed, and the girls' laughter just made it all the worst. Sandy let it be known immediately what he saw, but of course, the girl denied it. Bea rushed to the aid of her employee, while Big Al stepped through the revolving door that separated the kitchen from the serving bar in case Bea needed him.

Jon coughed and gagged, trying to catch his breath. Apparently, some of the water went down the wrong way. He was embarrassed, not because of Lily, but because at this particular minute he was having a hard time trying to act manly in front of the girls. Bea raised her voice and asked the troublemakers to leave—a move she would later regret immensely. Lily crawled out of Jon's lap and rushed back through the revolving door. Bea instructed the boys to get another booth, and Big Al quickly mopped up the water.

"Honey, it's all right. Don't you fret one bit." Bea tried her best to console the young lady, all the while the boys continued to eat from the basket of crackers that spilled onto the table.

"I'm hungry. When's she coming back?" Sandy asked.

Bea escorted Lily to the customers, and before long, their meal was on the table. The eight-year-old had trouble keeping his eyes on his food and off the pretty young waitress. Seconds before Lily brought them the check, Jon noticed a foul odor.

"What is that smell?" Jon whispered into Sandy's ear.

Sandy just giggled and said, "Whoever smelt it, dealt it."

It did not take her long to smell the odor for herself. She reached into her apron pocket and, without drawing much attention, eased the tissue up to her nose.

Sandy pointed at Jon. "He did it."

Jon reached across the table in an effort to grab the escaping prankster, but Sandy proved too fast, and as a last resort, Jon yelled, "Get in the truck."

$$$

On their way home, the boys could hear the siren of an ambulance off in the distance. Sandy begged to follow the sound. They were getting closer and closer to the sirens when they came upon the accident. Jon recognized the car immediately. Unbeknownst to Jon, Billy Wade Thompson and Pete McElhaney were first responders, and they began to shout orders to him.

"We need help getting the door unstuck," they both shouted.

The car's impact against the pine tree made the task difficult. Right away, Jon could smell the fumes from the leaking gas tank. He made the mistake of looking into the car.

"Oh God!" Jon had never seen that much blood and released his hands from the door, bending down to throw up the meal he had just eaten.

"Son, get back up here and help us with this door," Pete demanded.

There was no time to waste as smoke began to pour out from under what was left of the hood. The boys managed to pry the door open enough for the paramedic to get the collar around Stephanie's neck. Even with all the chaos surrounding him, as he and the sheriff stood watching the scene unfold, Jon was surprised at how eerily quiet it was. He watched as the paramedics placed the oldest Garvin girl's lifeless body on the gurney and watched as the helicopter landed on the highway. Trees blocked any attempt to open the passenger's side doors. Both girls in the back were moaning, which only made Jon more nervous.

Billy Wade checked the passenger in the front seat and shouted to the returning paramedic, "This one doesn't have a pulse."

No matter how hard they tried to revive the child, Elisabeth Garvin was not to be saved. She would forever remain eighteen. As she lay still on the ground, her beautiful blond hair gently moved in the breeze.

Sheriff Davis draped the cover over her head. He would have the difficult task of informing her parents, a job he found unbearable.

"How many times have I told these girls to slow down?" he shouted as his emotions begin to rise.

Jon stood speechless as the men continued to do the work they were trained to do.

"You can't get it to sink into their heads sometimes," McElhaney added and placed his arm around the shoulders of the uniformed man.

Billy Wade just shook his head at the loss.

A short moment of silence was followed by the screams of Mrs. Garvin. She had been waiting for the traffic to resume, unaware that the tragedy ahead involved her until she passed the scene herself. The deputies caught the woman as she stumbled down the embankment.

"Oh God. No! No!" She fell to her knees begging. "Not my babies! Not my babies!"

Jon stepped away from the scene and threw up once more. Billy Wade approached, "You all right, son?"

The ride home remained quiet. The tragic event was too much for Jon, not to mention Sandy. Eleanor thought it best if the lad stayed with her for the night. Jon woke during the night not only to the flashbacks of the girls' accident but also the one he was involved in when he was sixteen. At the time, he did not think much about crashing the new car his father had just bought him, but tonight, he realized he could have ended up just like Elisabeth. He could not even recall telling his father he was sorry about the car. Instead, he blamed the accident on another car, and with the high-priced lawyers involved, a settlement reached out of court with nothing remaining on his record. His father warned him many times about driving too fast, but he did not listen either.

$$$

Elisabeth's funeral, held in Jackson, was even sadder than the one for Sandy's mother. As Jon sat through the service, his mind shifted back to the accident. Over the next few weeks, the trauma was proving to be too much for everyone. Adding to it was the fact no one knew for sure if Stephanie would even recover from her head injury. A group of church members took turns relieving the distraught parents at the hospital. The Anderson sisters believed tragedies came in threes, and they were praying harder than ever.

When the doctor and Mrs. Garvin finally split for good, it did not surprise anyone. Lily volunteered to keep Anna when needed. He was overwhelmed, juggling his practice and dealing with the stress of his divorce, not to mention Stephanie's deteriorating condition. Jon did not know it at the time, but the Garvin's separation would affect him personally in the months to come.

The New Girlfriend 13

As the holidays drew closer, everything slowly returned to normal. Sam's slight cough worried only Evie. Eleanor wondered if Jon was still counting the days. Henry declared things were right on schedule to sell calves in the spring, and he thought Jon was doing well with the farm.

With Christmas within reach, Sandy talked about what he wanted from Santa. Henry picked at the child nonstop about the farm being too far away from the North Pole. With everyone planning, this Christmas would surely be the best ever for the young man.

Sandy was sitting at Eleanor's kitchen table in the RV, finishing his homework. Eleanor retired to her tiny room in the RV for the evening, giving the lad lights-out-at-nine instructions. Jon and Lily were on a double date with Sam and Caroline in Hattiesburg. Sandy once rebelled when Lily started taking up too much time with Jon; but now the lad had something, or rather someone, occupying his mind, and he did not dwell on the new couple as much. Not to mention, ever since seeing his teacher go into labor at school, Sandy stayed far away from Caroline.

$$$

The two couples found themselves at Antonio's again, a new Italian restaurant one town over, and Caroline's favorite food now. Her belly was practically growing inches in front of everyone's eyes, but no one dared to comment on that fact. The emotional mother-to-be was tired of being the size of two elephants, as she put it. Evie Rogers, grandmother-to-be, had everything ready.

All Caroline had to do now was spit that baby out. The daily but well-meaning phone calls from everyone in town were getting on Caroline's last nerve. "If one more person asks me if I've had this baby yet, I'm going to scream. Can't they see it is still there?" She points to her belly. "I mean, am I really this big normally?" Sam tried to calm her down. "Honey, they were only being nice."

The latest outburst was in reference to one of the church members who just happened to be dining at the restaurant.

Jon, trying to change the subject, spoke up, "Hey, guys, they just put another pan of pizza out." Jon rose to get a slice of the hot pizza from the buffet table. Sam followed.

"Get me a piece," Caroline demanded.

Jon's mistake came when he said aloud, "Seriously?"

Even the older couple in the next booth ducked their heads a little upon hearing the comment.

But it was too late. The damage had been done, and everyone in the place heard the very tired and very pregnant woman begin her emotional downfall right in the middle of the Friday night crowd. "You call your daddy right now. I want this thing out!" Her slow but deep voice gave everyone in the room a chill. "I've had enough!" She continued standing to give her more strength, as she began to throw silverware at the man who put her in this condition.

Caroline stopped her tantrum just as quickly as she started. Jon and Lily bent down on the floor, retrieving the forks and wiping up spilled soda. It was less embarrassing down there, not to mention safer being out of range of the silverware's flight. "Are you okay, honey?" Sam asked, as everyone in the restaurant waited on her next move.

"I think." She paused, and Jon took a chance to reach for the remaining fork located next to Caroline's right shoe. "I think."

Everyone, including the cashier, remained tense waiting for her to finish her sentence. Lily placed the plates back on the table and slowly sat back down in her chair, as Jon used the last of the napkins to soak up the spill at her feet.

"My water broke!"

Everyone gasped, everyone except Jon.

In the chaos of the situation, Sam left without paying the bill. In years past, this would have been no problem for Jon and his dad's credit card, but it was on this day. He would not be paid until Friday, and Sam was going to pick up this check. Jon had no alternative but to ask Lily for the money, a move that made him feel most uncomfortable.

$$$

Doctor Garvin was notified that Caroline was on the way. He was on call, making rounds with little Anna at his side. Next, Sam called his father at home. Evie was taking a dessert to the new couple that recently moved into the community. The doctor could not remember their names, and due to his anxiety about the coming grandchild, he had to focus on recalling his wife's cell phone number. Minutes passed as he dialed and redialed wrong numbers. By mistake, he dialed Caroline's phone then Sam's.

"Dad, you want me to call Momma?"

In the confusion, no one actually called her.

A nurse instructed Sam that first babies were usually slower to make their presence known. "Doctor Garvin will be in soon. He is finishing rounds, and it looks like you are going to be here a while. Try to relax."

The nurse allowed Jon and Lily to visit for just a few moments. Jon entered the hospital room waving a white napkin in the air. After all, it was his comment that started this mess tonight. Jon became nervous with all the machines beeping and departed to the safety of the waiting room. Lily was sitting at his side when she noticed Dr. Garvin walking by.

"Steve," she said, getting his attention.

Anna was happy to see her babysitter. "Lily!" she squealed.

"Jon, Lily," the doctor spoke as he shook Jon's hand.

"How long do you think this will take?" Jon asked.

"First babies are hard to call."

"You need me to watch Anna?" Lily asked.

Jon realized his date night was now over. "If you can, I think she's getting a bit hungry. Will you take her down to eat? Here's my card."

Lily stuck her hand out and informed the doctor, "No problem, buying supper is something I certainly know how to do." She cut her eyes toward Jon causing him to become embarrassed.

$$$

Meanwhile, back at Red Clay, Evie thought it would be a good idea to rent a movie before returning home for the evening. She had done everything on her mile-long list of things to do and could now use some quiet time. As she wheeled her car into the rental store parking lot, Pete McElhaney was getting into his truck.

"Woman, I thought you would be at the hospital by now."

She walked a little closer to him because some teenagers had their music turned up too loudly, preventing her from hearing the entire sentence. "What did you say about the hospital?"

It became obvious to him that she had not heard the news. "Now, Evie, don't you go getting upset, okay? Jon called me about an hour ago. Caroline went into labor."

Just as Pete predicted, Evie reacted badly to the news, and before she reached the hospital, the Mississippi Highway Patrol issued her one warning and one citation.

$$$

Everyone was exhausted by the time the eight-pound-twelve-ounce baby boy arrived.

James Brinson Rogers made his appearance into the world shortly before noon. Lily had long since left the hospital with Anna, driving the doctor's new car. She would return later that afternoon to take the doctor home. Lily loved the smell of a new car and could not stop talking about it. In fact, Lily was talking more and more about the doctor and his money and less and less about Jon.

The Trees   14

Sam waited patiently on the delivery truck from Hattiesburg every day. He knew he would not be there when the truck came in and gave specific instructions to call if they arrived while he was at the hospital with the new baby. Everyone in town, especially at the feed store, was excited about those trees, a little tired of talking about pecans but excited nonetheless.

$$$

The new father peered through the glass window into the nursery at the eight-pound-twelve-ounce baby boy. It had been a long night, and both men were tired.

Jon noticed for the first time that his friend looked pale. "You're white as a ghost."

Sam took a deep breath. "I think I need to eat something." With all the excitement, he had forgotten to eat and was very tired.

Evie passed them both as she made her way through the hospital hallway carrying a big blue wreath for the door and a handful of balloons attached to a giant bear. It was the first of many things Evie would be purchasing for her first grandchild. "Sam, why are you so pale?" she asked and insisted he lie down at once.

"I'm just tired, Mom. On our way to eat now." The two men stepped onto the elevator, and just as the door closed, Sam fainted. When they reached the first floor, Jon, with the help of the few men waiting for the elevator, carried him to find help. Within minutes, the emergency room doctors and nurses were busy trying to find out what was happening to the young man. Jon could not understand all that was being said, but when the nurse said something about a low blood pressure, he ran all the way back to Caroline's room to find Evie.

There was not enough hospital staff to keep Evie out of that ER room. She watched as the doctors shouted instructions to the nurses. For the first time in a very long time, Evie was at a loss for words and stood frozen, helpless. How many times had she been on the other side of the situation and for years been the one shouting orders and performing the tasks? But this was her own child. And coupled with the already emotionally draining events of the day, she was just overwhelmed. Amidst the chaos of the room, Jon truly and from his heart prayed to God for the very first time. He became weak in his knees and eased down to the floor. He listened through the curtains as the medical team worked on his best friend. Most of what was being said only confused him. Tears welled up in his eyes as he awkwardly talked to God.

Before long, someone shouted, "He's awake!"

Another nurse shouted out, "Ninety over sixty." Evie closed her eyes and thanked Jesus aloud.

After the doctor finally convinced the overprotective mother that he thought everything was going to be okay with her son, she gave the patient a thorough talking to about eating properly and getting plenty of fluids and getting his rest.

Since he was so weak and his blood pressure still a little low, Sam would need to stay in the hospital to rest and receive IV fluids. The doctor wanted to run a few tests while he was there anyway. Jon realized once again that his best friend was still sick and his future uncertain.

$$$

Jon was tired but did not want to go home. Instead, he chose to go to the feedstore, knowing it was almost time for the two o'clock delivery truck to arrive. Everyone was saddened to hear about Sam. Each one trying to do their part to help—Pete was going to visit, while Janice was organizing future meals. And of course, everyone was praying. The delivery driver rang the outside bell himself when he realized no one was coming to sign the invoice. The driver opened the door, revealing Sam's pecan trees. Janice sat at the front counter watching the men bring in the trees one by one passed the door. It was on everyone's mind. Even though Sam never complained and always was so optimistic, his future was still uncertain, and this little scare brought the reality back. Sam was loved by everyone in the community, and most were there when he was born.

The Wilson brothers left Jon to lock up for the day. In the quietness of the store, Jon sat alone, not knowing what to do next. He was angry the trees had come today and not yesterday so that Sam could have seen them. Sam was at the store every day to see what the truck was bringing. It did not make any sense to Jon. He began to question the God he had been worshipping at church. As he thought about his friend's battle with cancer, he shouted to the heavens, "I want to know why you did this to Sam? Tell me why!"

The knock on the feedstore door startled Jon. It was Pastor Johnson.

"Hey, Jon. I was driving by, going to check on the Anderson sisters, and had this overwhelming feeling that I needed to stop in here. I wasn't even sure anyone was still here."

Jon took a deep breath, trying to contain the anger that was rising in his throat. "Well, pastor, it's like this. Sam is in the hospital. The baby came, and the trees are here. And why, if God is so great and wonderful and all?"

The pastor listened as the questions poured out of the angry man.

"Sam is good. This should happen to bad people"—he paused— "like me, not Sam."

The pastor stayed quiet, trying to follow Jon's troubled ramblings as best he could. "I thought the chemo had worked again," the pastor responded.

Jon continued, "It did. I think, but he is weak, and his blood pressure is low. Why is he being punished? He is a good person."

"Jon, I know this is a difficult thing to understand," the pastor explained, "but God's plan may be different from ours. We may not know all the answers, but I do know two comforting truths—you are not alone and God loves you unconditionally."

The pastor went on. "Jon, death is not the punishment, son, if you believe. For without death on earth, you cannot get to your eternity." Jon looked down at the floor as he listened to the words the pastor was saying.

"Our time on this earth is only a brief moment. Everyone will have a death, and everyone will have an eternity, Jon."

Silence filled the room as the pastor's words began to find their place within Jon's heart.

"I should get to the hospital. Is there anything else you want to talk about, Jon?"

He shook his head no.

"Well, you know where to find me if you do."

Jon remained at the counter long after the pastor had left. And soon, he found himself loading up as many trees as his truck could carry. For the first time in Jon's life, he decided to help someone unselfishly. No one had to ask, and there was no ulterior motive.

$$$

B.C. Lee and his boys were returning home from the Friday night ball game. Both his sons played football, and Jacob, the oldest, was being scouted by all the junior colleges. As they drove by Sam's farm, the younger of the boys noticed headlights shining across the field. B.C. slowed to a crawl as he removed the set of binoculars from the driver's side door.

"Well, I'll be—"

The boys took turns looking at the city boy's work. "It looks like he's asleep."

$$$

Jon awoke the next morning to the sound of Billy Wade's loud country voice. "Rise and shine, boy. Yer burnin' daylight."

Pete and James McElhaney handed the boy a cup of coffee. As he took the coffee, the men noticed Jon had blistered hands.

Pete spoke first, "Son, you won't be using any of these today," and he took the posthole digger out of his hand. "You had better get cleaned up. We can finish this."

James piped in, "We'll handle the rest of these trees."

But Jon was not giving up now. He was bargaining with God. He would change his ways, be a better person if God would just heal his friend. He grabbed the posthole digger out of Pete's hand and grabbed another tree. Everyone followed suit.

Unbeknownst to Jon, B.C. Lee had made a few calls at daylight, and before long, the field was full of men planting pecan trees. Meanwhile, Eleanor and Esther were busy themselves making enough food and sweet tea to feed everyone for lunch. It was a good day for Jon, blisters and all. As he continued planting, he would find himself glancing over the field of the hardworking men. He observed the fine qualities each man possessed. Growing up, he and his friends would often make fun of those who labored for a living. There was B.C. Lee, with a piece of straw hanging from the side of his lips, and his two boys working near. Jon envied their close relationship. James, the more serious of the McElhaney brothers, was always there with a free hand when someone, especially Pete, was about to drop something. Billy Wade worked harder than any two men did. Nothing made him more nervous than hospitals, and he welcomed the distraction the trees had brought. Henry drove up, bringing Sandy home from school just as the last hole was being dug. The men gathered around and solemnly watched as Jon took the honor of placing the last of the trees into place. Sandy helped brush the loose dirt into the hole and gently patted the ground tightly around the young trunk. Jon felt good inside.

Billy Wade thought it proper to say a few words to the "Man upstairs," and he bowed his head. "Father, I reckon You know what's goin' on down here. I ask that You bring that boy back home safely. He still has lots of things to take care of around here with the new baby and all." He paused and then continued, "That girl of mine will be heartbroken if'n you see fit to take him now, so I ask you to let him stay a lil' while longer. Amen."

Everyone echoed with his own "Amen."

A Christmas Like No Other 15

As the sun was setting on the tiny house, Jon and Sandy stretched their tired bodies out on the couch, watching the twinkling of the lights glowing brightly from the tree. They had walked for hours in the woods finding just the right tree to decorate. Although scarcely decorated, Sandy thought it was the prettiest one he had ever seen. Each Christmas in his past had always lacked sparkle, not to mention joy. Usually, the holidays brought nothing but undeserving stress in the child's life. As far back as he could remember, the joyful season seemed to put his mother in a state of depression, causing either no presents to be found under the tree on Christmas morning or a last-minute trip through the welfare system because of her drinking binges.

Sandy, if given the option, would have chosen no presents at all as long as he could snuggle alongside his mother, even if she were sleeping off a drunken state. However, this Christmas would be different, and the sparkle in his eyes revealed he knew it. Sandy was eating the last of the popcorn not needed for decorations on the tree when the phone rang.

"Merry Christmas!" Sandy shouted into the phone upon answering it. "Yes, sir, he's right here. Hold on," Sandy continued and then tossed the phone to Jon, overthrowing just a bit.

"Ouch!" Jon yelled as the cordless phone hit his head. "Hello." Jon took the phone into the next room so Sandy could not hear the conversation.

"Are you sure?" Jon questioned. "But what about his school and Christmas?"

Jon did not believe what the sheriff was saying. "That can't be good for Sandy. Isn't there anything we can do about it?" Jon listened as the sheriff continued to explain the situation.

"But what if he doesn't want to go?" Jon, caught off guard with the news, could not think quickly enough. "I mean, I understand that a father has rights, but if what you are saying is true, he just got out of the pen. How can that be better for him than us?"

Nothing Jon said to the sheriff would change the fact that Sandy's long-lost father was being released from jail and wanted his son back.

Sandy never had a clear understanding as to what happened to his daddy. Todd Henderson had been serving a five-year sentence on a drug conviction—a conviction Sandy's mother should have received for the drugs hidden in his truck had been hers. He had spent the years behind bars vowing to get revenge, but since his former wife was dead, he wanted nothing more than to rebuild his broken bond with his son.

Jon told Sandy the news, not really knowing what to expect.

After a few minutes of staring off into space, the child stated, "I think I want a puppy for Christmas." And with that, the young man sprang from the couch and exited the room for bed.

Jon heard him say his request one more time before closing his bedroom door. "Yep, a puppy."

$$$

Between Sandy's new Christmas request and the news of Sam's continuing recovery, Jon was busier than ever. Two shopping days to go until Christmas and still no puppy to be found. And not just any old puppy would do; it had to be a blue Weimaraner. Jon tried everywhere, including the Gulf Coast and Jackson. He had conceded defeat when, by chance, a preacher from Hattiesburg had car trouble outside of Bea's restaurant. Bea, being the kindhearted soul she was, volunteered Jon for the job.

"Bea said you needed a jump start," Jon said, causing the man in the faded overalls to bump his head on the hood.

"Oh, sorry, didn't mean to startle you," Jon apologized.

The preacher, Reverend J. C. Fordham, explained that for some reason, his battery died. He had jumper cables; he just needed some juice to get the car started.

Jon looked at the preacher's new truck. "Nice truck."

The reverend had just retired from Shady Grove Baptist Church, and the congregation had given him the truck for all the years of devoted service.

"Yep, just got it. My granddaughter was fooling around in it yesterday and ran the battery down. I thought once I jumped it off this morning and drove it awhile, it would be okay."

Sandy had come to see what was taking Jon so long. "I'm hungry."

Jon held his hand up to signal him to be quiet so he could hear the preacher explain about the jumper cables. All Jon had left to do was connect the jumper cables on the battery then wait for the preacher to crank his truck.

"Okay. Was it red on the left and black on the right?" Jon asked aloud.

Sandy was only adding to the confusion, for sleeping in the back seat of the truck was the prettiest puppy Sandy had ever seen. "Jon, Jon, Jon. Look!" Sandy tapped on the glass, awakening the pup and immediately fell in love with the blue-eyed, short-haired puppy stretched out on the back seat behind the driver's side.

"Did he say right?" Jon asked.

Sandy took off around the back of the truck to get a better look.

"Look, Jon, right there," Sandy yelled.

"The right side? Sandy, did he say the right side?" But the child was too excited to be of any good help.

"Yeah, right there, Jon. Right there!"

Sandy was, of course, talking about where the puppy was located and nothing in fact to do with the car trouble.

And since all Jon heard was the word *right*, he proceeded to damage the electrical system of the preacher's new truck. A little puff of black smoke, followed by some static noise, told Jon he had done it wrong.

The preacher slowly exited the truck cab, asking, "What was that noise?"

The very least Jon could do was offer the man a ride home. A tow truck would arrive later to remove the vehicle from Bea's parking lot and return it to the dealership in Hattiesburg.

"Well, young man, I appreciate the offer, but I need to deliver that dog first," the preacher explained. His daughter had puppies to deliver before Christmas, and he was helping.

"I really want a puppy," Sandy exclaimed. "Got anymore?"

Reverend Fordham, Sandy, the puppy, and Jon squeezed into the little Chevy S-10 for the forty-two mile trip to Carnes.

"I think that girl of mine may have one or two more for sale." He felt around in his overalls for his cell phone. "Hmmm, I must have left that phone of mine in the truck. I guess we'll just have to wait until you take me home to see if they have all sold."

Sandy held tightly around the pup's neck and talked to it all the way. Jon thought the gravel roads leading up to his own farm were bad, but those leading to the Puckett farm where the lil' pup was to be dropped off were almost impossible to travel.

"Son, you might want to have someone look at your shocks," the preacher advised as he held on tightly to the dashboard.

By the time they made it to the reverend's house, it was approaching six-thirty.

"You boys want to eat a bite of supper first?"

Jon was hungry, but Sandy could not wait any longer to see the puppies.

"That gal of mine should be at the barn. Help yourself. Supper will be ready when you finish." The preacher pointed to the smaller barn down the road. "See that light post there?"

Sandy ran all the way, leaving Jon all alone on the dark pathway.

By the time Jon arrived, Sandy had already made claim to the blue-colored female pup. The short, chubby girl wearing a baseball cap lacked beauty, to say the least, but she took an immediate liking to Jon.

"Just tell me how much, and we'll be out of your way," Jon said.

As Sandy rolled around in the scattered hay on the barn floor, Jon fought off the advances of the toothless girl.

"You sure are pretty. You married?" asked the country girl. He motioned for Sandy to get up.

"How, how much did you say?"

She twisted the greasy strand of hair hanging out of her baseball cap and grinned. "I'm willing to make a deal with you because you sure are pretty," she said.

Sandy was giggling as his new puppy licked his face.

"Look, they are kissing." The girl noticed. "I wish I had somebody to kiss me too," she said, moving closer and closer to the nervous Jon.

"Sandy!" Jon yelled. "We got to go now, son." Nevertheless, the child paid them no attention.

"Again, I must ask. How much is the puppy?" Jon took out his wallet.

The rejected girl took a couple of steps back and sat down on one of the hay bales surrounding the puppies.

"They are five hundred dollars, and I don't take checks."

Jon was floored. "Five hundred dollars! You've got to be kidding."

The girl winked at Sandy, who, upon hearing the price, had stopped playing with the dog.

"I said I was willing to make a deal with your daddy." Sandy looked up with pleading eyes.

Jon found himself hating to ask. "What kind of deal?"

"I'll take three hundred and a big kiss," she said and took off her baseball cap, waiting.

"Sandy," Jon motioned for the child to come over.

"What?"

"Give the lady a kiss so we can go."

"Uh-uh," declared Sandy. "No way!"

No matter how badly the child wanted that dog, a kiss was out of the question, especially a kiss with her.

"But I wasn't talking about the boy," informed the grinning woman, as she latched onto Jon, holding tightly around his neck.

Jon gagged all the way back to his truck, but Sandy paid no mind to the commotion.

The preacher was waiting on the front porch. "The wife, said Cassidy, would be back in a minute. You guys come on in."

"Uh, we spoke to your daughter down at the barn. Thanks for the offer, but we got to get going." Jon spit once more.

"Here comes my girl now." The dark-blue jeep pulled up next to the boys. "I see you got the blue one."

A very attractive girl with long brown hair leaped from the jeep.

Jon had a puzzled look on his face. "Then who was that back there?" Jon pointed to the barn.

"Short, homely girl?" the preacher asked.

Jon nodded yes.

"Daddy, she's doing it again," Cassidy told her father.

"Doing what again?" Jon inquired.

The preacher called for his wife through the screen door, "Martha, call down to the Thompson's and tell them to come get Nancy."

"Nancy is a little bit of a handful and loves to aggravate people. Folks around here call her the kissing bandit."

Cassidy bent down and patted Sandy's new puppy on the top of the head. "Be thankful you didn't have to kiss her."

"No, not me," Jon stated.

"Oh yes, you did," Sandy confessed.

Everyone laughed. Jon spit once more.

Cassidy 16

Cassidy Fordham had lived in the same house since birth. Ever since grade school, she wanted to be a veterinarian. Her father had preached at the same church as far back as she could remember. Being the preacher's kid always had its downside. Everybody thought she should be on her best behavior, which by her nature was hard to do. The tomboyish girl loved the outdoors and loved animals. Against her parents' wishes, she mostly hung with the boys. "All the girls want to do is play with dolls and put on makeup" was her constant defense.

Somewhere around the age of fifteen, one of the local boys became more than just a buddy. Cassidy delivered a baby girl three weeks shy of her sixteenth birthday. The young man's parents moved to the coast shortly after Cassidy revealed who the daddy of her baby was. The congregation nearly split over the matter. The preacher, in one of his best sermons, let everyone know God never makes mistakes, and while Emily's parents may not have followed the path God wanted them to, we cannot judge for we all have veered off that path. Of course, at the embarrassment of his daughter, he did go on to say sexual relations before marriage was biblically wrong and a sermon for another day.

Cassidy completed high school, but her dreams of higher education were limited to the junior college. The preacher loved his daughter but firmly believed it was her responsibility to tend to the child. Cassidy supported her baby by working at the local veterinarian clinic and received extra money from the sale of her puppies she raised. Emily's daddy wanted nothing to do with the child, and that turned out to be a blessing in disguise. Throughout the remainder of his teenage years, he spent most of it in trouble with the law, eventually ending up in jail for a short time.

$$$

Jon sat across the table from the young mother, but Sandy refused to put the puppy down and join the meal.

The preacher's wife yelled upstairs, "Emily, time to eat."

Before long, the four-year-old made her way down the oak staircase, tapping the bottom of her tap shoes on each step. *Tap-tap, tap-tap, tap-tap.*

"Emily! We have company. Stop that noise," the young mother pleaded to no avail.

Tap-tap, tap-tap.

"Emily, honey," the grandmother added.

Tap-tap, tap-tap, tap-tap.

"Young lady!" the preacher added in a raised voice.

Tap, tap, tap, tap, tap, tap. She hustled downstairs and jumped into her grandmother's lap.

The Revival   17

Life without Sandy was difficult at times. But Sam's release from his second admission to the hospital since the baby was born helped keep Jon busy, not to mention the puppy that was left behind. Sandy's new apartment would not allow animals. The boy's daddy promised they would return to visit on weekends. But the weeks were turning into months, and Jon was sure he and the dog would soon be forgotten.

$$$

It was Jon's time to drive the Anderson sisters up to Hattiesburg for their monthly doctor's visit, and he decided to surprise the young lad, but sadly, the apartment manager said they had moved out and left no forwarding address.

Jon was thankful it would be months before his turn to chauffer the old women again. Between the strong-perfumed powder the women wore on special occasions and the constant stops at the restrooms, Jon was mentally tired. Then of course, the grocery store was a fiasco. The women always fought over which of their meat-loaf recipes was the best and who was going to do the cooking for the upcoming Revival dinner. Each woman swore the visiting preacher had commented on her recipe.

"No, no, sister. It was *my* recipe, and remember you had come down with a case of gas, and I had all the cooking to do," Della said in front of the butcher.

Jon lowered his head in an attempt to keep from laughing at the woman's comment.

"Sister! I have never had gas that prevented me from serving the Lord," Stella insisted. "I specifically remember Pastor Fordham talking about *my* recipe, and his darling wife said she was sure he would remember it for a long time."

Jon interrupted the bickering women, "Did you say Fordham?"

Jon hurried the two women with their shopping as best he could. He had many things to do before the kickoff dinner, which he had just found out was always hosted the night before Revival was to start on Sunday. Jon needed to get the women back to Red Clay by six o'clock in the evening in order to make it to Mac's barbershop before he closed at six-thirty. Della insisted Jon slow down. She actually thought the car needed to cool down midway through the trip back home, but Jon insisted their Buick Electra 225 was just fine. Jon knew Stella's second glass of tea, and then the cup of coffee with her dessert, would only delay the ride home. And it did—twice. He practically pushed the women and their groceries through the front door of their home and had five minutes to get two miles down the road to the barbershop. Mac had just stepped outside and was about to lock the door when Jon slid into the parking lot.

"I need a cut, Mac!" he hollered out the window.

"Just closed, son." Mac pulled the key out of the door.

"Come on, Mac. I really need a favor," Jon pleaded.

"If only you could have been here two minutes earlier, but I've already set the alarm, and besides, Erma has supper on the table. Didn't you know I closed at six-thirty?"

"Yeah, I did, but Stella's bladder didn't."

"Anderson sisters?"

"Yeah. I was February."

"Well now, I think we might be able to work a little something out. You're looking at March here," said the grinning barber.

Jon got his haircut, and Mac no longer had to worry with a trip to Hattiesburg next month.

$$$

93

Jon found himself at the church thirty minutes early. He was waiting for Cassidy to arrive. The reverend and Mrs. Fordham had mentioned at the supper the night before that his entire family would be joining them for the upcoming services. Jon had found himself thinking about the long-legged country girl since the day he bought the puppy. Many times, he picked up the phone to call but could never get past Emily, who refused to tell her mother that Jon was calling. Even once, he had the privilege of talking to Nancy, which proved somewhat of a mistake. Nancy took Jon's number off the caller ID and called every day until her father received the next month's telephone bill. Even his genius plan to take the new puppy forty miles, past the two closer veterinarians' clinics, just to see her at work, failed when she had the day off. But now, this was his chance to reintroduce himself and maybe, just maybe, ask her out on a date. The music had already started when he made his move to the second row and slid in next to her. Emily recognized him instantly, and in a move proving to be smart, even for a four-year-old, she slid off her mother's lap and positioned herself in between them both.

Over the course of the next three sermons, Jon found himself less involved with Cassidy, Emily, or even Nancy, who had traveled with the Fordhams to the Revival. Something deep within Jon was struggling to come out. He had felt these very feelings several times before since moving to Red Clay, but Reverend Fordham's sermons seemed to be directed only at Jon. How did the man know his secret inner thoughts? He had been able to suppress the urge to respond, and with the last chorus of the invitation being sung, he knew he could resist the temptation, if you will, of walking down the aisle once more. Unlike in any sermon of Pastor Johnson, this visiting preacher took it upon himself to stop the verse in mid-sentence. As the piano player continued to play the hymn softly, the preacher opened his mouth, but to Jon, the words coming out seemed as if they were being spoken directly from the Almighty Himself.

"How many times will I have to make myself known to you before you truly acknowledge me? Was I not there when you needed me at the hospital?" Jon thought about Sam.

"Was I not there when you questioned my decisions about loved ones?"

Jon thought about his grandfather and, more recently, about Sandy's mother.

"Was I not there when you hit rock bottom and someone asked me to send help to you?" His father had hired Eleanor.

"Did I not show you love as only a child could love you?" God was surely talking about Sandy.

"Hasn't someone around you been praying faithfully for your very soul?"

Jon did not know who this could be and thought it was probably the Anderson sisters, who prayed for everyone in the state of Mississippi at times.

"Why not come now! Release the burdens that trouble your heart! Let me take them away!"

Jon felt mighty hands pushing him out of the pew. Was it God moving him? Was it God calling him by name?

Again, he heard his name.

"Jon! Move out of my way."

It was not God asking him to move, but none other than Nancy, feeling the need to rededicate her life to the Lord. With great force, she shoved the young man out into the aisle and made her way up to the waiting pastor.

Jon, left standing alone in the aisle, would make the greatest decision he would ever make in his life at this very moment.

One-Year Anniversary 18

Sam and Jon finished helping Henry load the cattle trailer for the trip to the stockyard. Spring was just around the corner, and this week had brought the first of many warm days to come. The young men were planning a day in Hattiesburg after delivering the cattle. This was a proud moment for Jon, selling his cattle to the highest bidder, and then the boys would head to the John Deere store to window-shop for Sam's new tractor. Jon had begun making plans to plow the back forty and plant Tifton Bermuda grass, a top-of-the-line hay enjoyed by the most pampered of horses. Over the winter, he realized many farms surrounding the Hattiesburg area were in need of good horse hay. He saw the opportunity to make a profit selling this hay to the weekend farmers, who owned small tracts of land in order to raise horses for their children's pleasure.

Since dating Cassidy, he would travel the forty miles to her house at least twice a week and then again on Sunday. Jon had begun to live this new life on his own. Eleanor had long since become just a neighbor, instead of the caretaker hired by his father. She and Henry had often wondered if Jon remembered this would be his last month before he inherited his money. Eleanor had seen the scrawny young man with spiked hair develop into a tanned, muscular country boy, who now had a fondness for cowboy hats and jeans. Eleanor thought even his father would have a hard time recognizing his own son. The small community of Red Clay had taken him in like the prodigal son returning from his wayward ways. And with the exception of Evie Rogers, no one knew about the fortune that lay waiting for the young man. All in Red Clay would soon know a secret promise she had made to her younger sister almost twenty-five years ago.

Returning Home 19

J. Marcus Howell Sr. stood in deep thought, gazing out over the blueness of the ocean. His cruise was about over and expected to be docking within the hour. Once again, his thoughts were on Jon, his only son. Had it worked? For a man totally in control of a business empire such as his, it was hard not knowing what had been taking place with his son over the past twelve months. Eleanor had threatened to quit when she found the private investigator snooping around Red Clay. Eleanor had her rules, and even money would not make her change her mind. Besides, in small towns, an outsider, especially a private investigator, sticks out like a sore thumb.

His thoughts wandered back to the days shortly after Rachel's death. He never quite felt welcomed into her close-knit family. Rachel's father Samuel Brinson never forgave J. Marcus for eloping with his youngest daughter.

Rachel's death only added fuel to the fire.

"You'll never amount to a hill of beans," Sam yelled at the then young J. Marcus. Anytime the two of them were in the same room, the sparks would fly.

"I'll be worth more than this whole county combined. You'll see!" J. Marcus, at the time, was taking the biggest chance of his life, borrowing more money to invest in an already sinking company. The chance paid off after a few years, but at the time, he had no idea what the future would hold, and the stress of the new baby was more than any man could handle. Rachel's oldest sister offered to raise the infant, but the hatred between J. Marcus and Sam Brinson prevented any chance of that happening. Rachel's sister pleaded with the feuding men to think of the child. Jon's mother had made her sister promise to help take care of her baby if she did not make it.

"Shhh. Don't talk like that. You are going to be okay." The young nurse tried to encourage her sister.

"Promise me you'll help Marcus." The older girl could only shake her head yes. "I need to hear you say it, Evie," Rachel pleaded.

The young doctor who had been standing at the bedside with Evie took Rachel's hand. "We both will. You have my word."

Rachel smiled and asked to see her baby once more.

$$$

The words over the loudspeaker startled Marcus back to the present. He wiped the escaping tears and looked down at his watch. "Two more days."

He could not wait to see if his plan had worked. Eleanor had finally given him permission to come to Red Clay, and he did not want to waste any time getting there.

$$$

Mary Alice Hartford had been his secretary going on fourteen years. She was surprised to hear his voice on the phone. Since her boss had been out of the office, she had missed him greatly.

"Mary Alice! How the heck are you?"

"Is that you, Marcus?" The call had a little static.

"You betcha. Get me on the first flight down to Mississippi tomorrow."

"Did you say Mississippi?"

"That's right, honey."

"Well, halleluiah! It is time to see Jon! Did it work? What does he look like?"

Mary Alice was full of questions.

"Well, hold your horses, girl. I haven't seen that boy in almost a year. But if that woman did her job, I know he'll be just fine."

$$$

Since becoming a permanent fixture at the Fordham home, Martha had taken a liking to her daughter's new beau. J.C., on the other hand, was not as thrilled mostly because the accident-prone young man was very interested in his youngest child and then there were the many mishaps that seem to follow Jon around like a shadow, starting with the damage to his new truck, followed by the day Jon accidentally walked through Martha's new back screen door, ripping the screen in half. Thankfully, Martha had witnessed the entire event, claiming that Emily had on purpose slammed the door into Jon and the boxes he had been carrying. Although the reverend found the story very suspicious, he did not fuss too much when Martha insisted he replace the door that evening before the weekly Baptist women's meeting, which she always hosted on the first Tuesday of every month. Perhaps one of the funniest moments to Martha was when J.C. and Jon decided to catch Saturday night supper from the catfish pond. Despite Sam's best efforts at teaching Jon to fish, it was almost impossible to have an accident-free fishing experience. Although much better than when he first came to Red Clay, Jon still lacked complete control of the pole or, rather, one would say, the lure. For that evening, J.C. required a trip to the local medical clinic to remove the lure from his arm and then to the doctor the following Monday for a new pair of eyeglasses. Thankfully, the preacher was well learned in the Bible because his notes on Sunday's sermon were useless without his glasses. Martha, as usual, defended Jon by saying the fish from Pop's Fish House was even better than her recipe and a lot less mess in her kitchen.

Emily still had not warmed up to the outsider and attempted to push him out of the picture, involving Nancy whenever possible. In spite of the odds, Jon never gave up on dating Cassidy or getting on the good side of the preacher. When Pastor Johnson asked Jon whom he wanted to do the honor of baptizing him, of course, Jon chose J.C. Fordham. The upcoming event would be taking place during the next Sunday's evening service. The Anderson sisters were in charge of refreshments, honoring the five new souls who recently dedicated their lives to the Lord. Arrangements had been made so that J.C.

and his family could attend the evening service at Red Clay Baptist Church. Both he and Pastor Johnson would go into the baptistery.

$$$

In a bold way but true to his nature, J. Marcus reentered town like he had promised years before, with more money in his pocket than the entire town combined. Eleanor insisted he could not make himself known until after the baptism; she wanted nothing to interfere with the occasion. He reluctantly agreed, and besides, the two remaining days would be spent making his sister-in-law Evie's life as miserable as possible, of course, only for fun. He wanted nothing more than to rekindle his once great relationship with her—a relationship ruined when Evie had to choose between her daddy and him.

He waited until five minutes until closing time to walk into the clinic. He was trying hard not to grin from ear to ear and began to fill out the paperwork Caroline's replacement had handed him. Evie had just counted the last of the medications in the drug cabinet, a routine procedure done at the beginning and end of every shift, when the secretary placed the new chart onto Evie's desk.

"Who's that coming in at the last minute? Tell them we already closed up for the day."

The newest employee turned to go and tell the man the news.

"Oh, never mind, I'll do it. What's wrong with him anyway?" She sounded aggravated.

"A pain in the neck? Send him back." Evie knocked on her husband's door. "We got one more."

"Be right out." The doctor was finishing his calls to the hospital.

Evie was reaching into the cabinet to retrieve a paper gown for her late arrival, when a familiar voice from the past spoke, "Hello, Evie."

$$$

The three of them sat in the doctor's office. Evie could not decide whether to slug or hug the grinning man. The doc finally asked, "Have you seen him?"

"No, not yet."

"Why didn't you let us know he was coming?" Evie started the first of many questions.

"It was all part of this deal I had with this lady," Marcus answered.

"Eleanor?"

Marcus nodded yes.

"I told Doc something strange was going on with that woman. I almost spilled the beans when I saw that scar on his back, but he didn't seem to know who we were, so I kept quiet for a little while to see what kind a scam you were up to."

"No scam, just eating crow, that's all," J. Marcus confessed.

"Why haven't you seen him yet?" Evie wanted to know.

"Can't, until Sunday night."

"What do you mean, can't?" the doc asked.

"All part of the plan," J. Marcus confessed.

"What plan?" Evie and the doc asked at the same time.

"You'll see. What you got for supper?" J. Marcus changed the subject, and soon, the trio was en route to the Rogers's home for a good old-fashioned meal unlike J. Marcus had not had in quite some time.

The Reunion 20

Doc walked over to his wife's brother-in-law waiting across the street from the church. Services would soon start, and J. Marcus waited patiently for the first glance of his son. J. Marcus listened as Doc pointed out a few of the original members, some he remembered vividly, while others remained unclear.

"The Anderson sisters?" J. Marcus recalled the two frail women getting out of a car.

"None other," the doc confirmed.

"I thought they would be dead and gone by now," J. Marcus added.

"I think they are going to outlive us all."

"Nothing seems changed."

"What do you mean? I have you know Red Clay has moved into the twenty-first century," said the doc, defending his little town.

"I mean, it's still the same church, the same old feed and seed store, the post office is still in the same place, and I bet Barney's sons are running his garage," the returning man guessed.

"Yep, but we have that video store now and Velma's fingernail and hair salon down on East Main."

"What happened to Lounette's beauty shop?"

Back in his day, Lou's was the place to hear all the gossip in town.

"Lounette had a stroke while giving someone a perm. Now let me think who that was. Oh yeah, Betty Maxwell. It took her months before her hair laid down right. The sheriff ordered Mac—

you remember the barber—to get those perming things out of Betty's hair."

"Betty Maxwell, the piano teacher?"

"Yep. Do you know how hard it was on Sundays to keep from laughing at that poor woman's head of hair? I'll give it to her. She kept right on playing that piano, never missed a service."

"There he is." The doc noticed Jon coming around the side of the church.

"Where?"

"Right there. Going up the steps," the doc said and pointed at him.

"Him? Right there?"

"Yep."

J. Marcus watched in silence while Jon opened the door for a couple of women and a small child. Doc thought he saw tears come to the eyes of J. Marcus.

"I didn't recognize him."

"Yep. He sure has changed a good bit since coming here."

"He looks good, don't he?" The father was proud. "Gained a few pounds, though."

"Yep. Twenty-eight to be exact, although he hasn't been into the clinic in the past couple of months."

"And that hair. It's normal hair."

"Yep, although that took a while. He and Sandy had that episode with the lice first."

"Sandy?" Doc forgot that J. Marcus had no knowledge of the past twelve months regarding his son.

"Oh yeah. Sandy was like a foster child."

"Who in their right mind would give my child a kid to raise?"

"You ready to go in?" Doc asked.

"Remember all those times Rachel tried her best to get me inside this church?"

"Yep," Doc remembered.

"I have been so wrong so many times and just too darn stubborn to admit it."

"Yep, but Evie never gave up praying for you and that boy. Every day." He paused to let J. Marcus go through the door first. "Every day," he said again.

J. Marcus sat on the back row, watching every move his son made during the service, noticing how at ease his now-grown son had become. The two women and small child he had seen walking with Jon were now sitting beside him. The familiar faces of the congregation flooded J. Marcus with many memories—some good, some sad—many were of his lovely wife. He found himself reliving past sermons instead of listening to the present one. As the preacher called for those needing baptizing to leave the sanctuary, one of the Anderson sisters suddenly noticed the stranger sitting alone on the back row. Della nudged Stella to look.

Stella, with the help of her walker, stood up in the choir to get a better look. "I think you're right, Della."

Long since being able to whisper in church, she said it loud enough for her sister and everyone on the first few rows to hear.

"Is that you, Jeffrey?" Stella yelled to the back of the church as she was making her way out of the choir loft.

"It's not Jeffrey. It's James," Della corrected her sister just as loudly.

Evie shook her head at the commotion taking place. Pastor Johnson looked over at the minister of music to do something.

Stella made it to the pew just as Della stood up and yelled, "I believe the name is Jon Marcus."

Evie eased out of her pew and escorted Stella into the back row. By the time the Reverend J.C. Fordham appeared in the baptistery, every one of the congregation had turned looking at the visitor, who could do nothing other than stand and say, "Jonathan Marcus Howell Sr., pleased to meet you all," and he sat back down.

Once Evie informed Stella of what was going on, they sat next to J. Marcus in time to see Jon's baptism.

The entire congregation said, "Amen!"

Eleanor, Esther, and Martha each wiped a tear from their eyes. Soon, Jon and the others changed from wet clothes and made their way into the fellowship hall for refreshments. It was there for the first time in a year that Jon spotted his father, sitting at the table with the doc, Evie, Sam, and Caroline.

J. Marcus stood up to greet his approaching son.

"Dad!"

"Jon Marcus."

"I just go by Jon now. What are you doing here?"

"Well, is that any way to greet your father? It has been a year, you know?"

"I mean, what about Eleanor?" Jon asked, but his father laughed a little.

"A year?" Jon realized for the first time the year was over.

Eleanor approached the conversation.

"It looks like I got my money's worth, Mrs. Sims." He reached to shake her hand.

"I should say so. I can't take all the credit myself. This town had a lot to do with it." She pointed to the small crowd of folks who had gathered around the table.

"Oh, Dad. This is Doctor and Evie Rogers, their son Sam, his wife Caroline, their child Brinson. Over here is—"

J. Marcus interrupted, "Son, I know all these great people. Here, let me introduce them to you. This is your Aunt Evie and your uncle. Evie here is your mother's sister. And this is your little cousin Sam. And that little bundle of joy right there, I believe, is named after your grandfather, Sam Brinson."

Evie nodded yes.

"Cousin?" both Sam and Jon said in unison.

Evie and J. Marcus laughed.

Jon sat down to hear the rest of the story.

Pete McElhaney walked over to the table. "J. Marcus, is that really you?" The men shook hands.

"Afraid so, Pete."

"Long time no see."

"Too long. Too long," J. Marcus agreed.

"I thought this had to be your son, but Evie threatened to tar and feather us if we mentioned anything. He's a fine young man. You should see what he did with Uncle Sam's old place."

"Uncle Sam?" Jon was getting more confused as the conversation continued.

"That's right, son. Evie and I are first cousins."

"You all knew?" Jon asked.

"I didn't," Sam confessed.

"I didn't until you gained all that weight. You started looking more and more like Uncle Sam," Pete informed Jon.

"I didn't until Evie told me," Doc stated. "Although I should have guessed, you are just as accident prone as your father was back then." Everyone laughed.

"Evie was the only one who knew almost immediately. That scar on your back you got when she was watching you while your old man was out west on his honeymoon with that stepmom of yours. Speaking of her, where is Amanda?" the doctor asked.

"Oh, just another bad case of judgment on my part. She's been long gone," confessed J. Marcus.

"Jon, it looks like that sweet thing from down south is leaving now," Pete interrupted to inform the guest of honor.

"Yeah, son, who is that girl?" J. Marcus asked.

"What?" Jon darted toward the door to speak to her before she left, but Della Anderson wouldn't make her new walker move fast enough, and he missed telling her goodbye.

J. Marcus made his way through the town visiting all of Rachel's relatives and even stopping by the Anderson sisters for late afternoon coffee.

As night fell, J. Marcus found himself on a grand tour of the old homeplace. Pete had been right. Jon had done a good job restoring the old farmhouse. The senior Howell paused at the doorway of his first wife's childhood bedroom. "This was the room your mother and Evie shared. I remember it had gigantic pink flowers on the wallpaper." Jon had chosen the very room of his mother.

"I saw them. We had a time getting that wallpaper off the wall, so in some places, we just painted over them with thick white primer."

"You don't say?" The father was surprised to hear this type of comment coming from his own son.

"Yep."

"So it's been good here?" the father asked.

"Yep."

"Is this Sandy?" the father noticed a few pictures stuck on the refrigerator door with homemade magnets.

"Yeah."

"Where is he?"

"Don't know." Jon straightened one of the pictures. "You want something to drink?"

"Yes! What do you got?" J. Marcus had needed a drink since returning to this town.

"Coke and some of Esther's sweet tea."

"Nothing a little harder?"

"Not in this town," Jon laughed.

"I guess some things will never change."

The two men were silent for a few minutes, as J. Marcus continued to look around the place.

"I can't wait to see this place in the daylight hours."

"Yeah."

The men walked to the porch. J. Marcus stared out into the darkness and listened to the sounds of the country life—sounds he had long forgotten.

"So, son, are you ready to go home?" the father finally asked, as Jon finished the last of his Coke.

The conversation was interrupted by car lights entering the driveway. Eleanor was about to get down to business. Her job had been accomplished, and she was ready to start her retirement.

"I'm handing over the keys to your RV and the truck," Eleanor informed Jon.

"My RV?"

"Yes. I thought you could use it while remodeling this old place," the father added. "And every good farm needs a good truck and a big tractor, don't you think?" he added.

Jon looked over at Eleanor. "My RV? My truck? A tractor?"

Eleanor grinned. "You never asked." She shrugged her shoulders, defending her position about the RV and the new truck that Henry drove.

"Is something wrong, son?" The father was not following the conversation.

"Tractor?" Jon asked Eleanor.

Eleanor explained that buying the new equipment might have hindered the process. She thought it best for Jon to work for what he needed. She had been right.

"Oh yeah." She dug into her purse to retrieve the keys to the tractor. "Here they are."

Jon took the keys from her hand and started laughing.

She turned to J. Marcus and said, "I believe you have a little something for me."

He reached into his dress coat pocket and placed two envelopes into her hand.

She opened the one addressed to her first and thanked him for his business, placing the check into her oversized purse. The other envelope she presented to Jon.

"I have to admit, I had my doubts at first. Frankly, I thought you might accidentally kill yourself before you got the hang of this farm. Nevertheless, I think you have grown into a fine young man with a good future ahead of you. Whether you decide to leave Red Clay or stay, you will be all right."

Jon took the envelope containing a check for his full inheritance. She hugged him tightly and walked toward the door.

"You are leaving? Just like that?" Jon asked.

"Yep."

She finally allowed herself to use the country slang and laughed at how it sounded coming from her mouth.

"I got a retirement calling my name. Oh, and one more thing"— she turned to J. Marcus and asked him—"did you find that little thing I asked you about?"

"Yes. It should be here any moment." J. Marcus confined. "Good then, and by the way, you look pretty good for a dead man."

"Yeah, about that." He tried to confess he had lied, but she already knew.

"No need." She hugged Jon once more and departed, leaving Jon and his father alone. Just like that, she was gone.

"You never did answer the question," J. Marcus asked again.

"What question?"

"Are you ready to go home?"

Jon thought a minute and began to speak, "I—" His sentence stopped again but this time by the sound of a car horn honking in the distance. Through the darkness, they could see the flashing of the sheriff's blue lights.

"What's going on now?" Jon was concerned. The two men headed out to the yard to meet the sheriff as he turned into the drive.

"Jon, I believe I found something that belongs to you," he said. The sheriff walked around to the passenger side of the car. At first, the headlights were blinding Jon's view of what the sheriff had gotten from the car, but as the man stepped closer to the front porch, Sandy came into full view. "Sandy!" Jon rushed over to the child, almost stumbling.

"Jon!"

"What happened to you?" Jon noticed the cast on the child's arm.

The sheriff spoke up, informing Jon that the boy and his father were involved in an accident that killed a man. The father was in intensive care, and Sandy wanted to stay with Jon until he got out of the hospital.

"If the father makes it, he will be facing vehicular manslaughter charges, and God only knows when he will get the boy again," the sheriff whispered to the men.

Jon introduced Sandy to J. Marcus, and the three of them talked late into the night until Sandy fell asleep, lying on the floor next to his dearly missed dog.

It was good to have Sandy around the farm again. Bright and early, both boys were tending to the animals. Jon had missed the child, especially his help with the chickens. Sandy counted the chickens twice just to make sure they were still all there.

"Eight red, five black, and white speckled, six black and one red rooster."

"All there," Jon confirmed.

"Yep, all there."

Sandy threw the birds a handful of corn. He would come back later in the day to gather the eggs. The cows had become accustomed to being fed early in the morning.

"Hey, where are all the cows?" Sandy had already left when Jon had sold some of the older cows at the stockyard. Henry had said to keep a few of the younger stock to replace some of the older herd.

"Hey, where's the bull?"

Jon sold that too.

"I needed to get a new bull because of the younger cows. Maybe this week we can go get one." Jon was still making plans about the farm, not giving into the fact he might be leaving now.

"How about one of those Brahma bulls like at the McElhaney farm?" That bull was the envy of all the farmers around.

"Can't get one of them just yet," Jon confessed.

"Why not?" asked Sandy.

"They cost a good deal."

"Oh."

The two of them walked closer to the house.

"Hey, why is Eleanor's house in our yard?"

"She's gone to retirement."

"That doesn't mean she is dead, does it?" Sandy asked to make sure.

"No, just her job is through."

"What job?" the boy questioned.

Jon was about to answer when it hit him.

"Hey! Go get dressed. We are going to get a bull—a Brahma bull."

"A Brahma bull like the McElhaney's bull?"

"Yep, and some cows, and a boat for that pond down there, and a steak from Hattiesburg."

"Huh?" Sandy said with a look of bewilderment.

Jon heard the phone ringing as they approached the house. It was Cassidy calling. His father answered before he could get his boots off and get to the phone.

"I see," his father said. "I see," he said again. "You don't say. Okay then, we will see you at six," he said and hung the phone up.

111

Jon waited while his father poured himself a cup of coffee. "And?"

"Excuse me?" J. Marcus added.

"The phone?"

"Oh, we have a date. Six o'clock. Fordham place. Nothing formal." His father smiled a little before sipping his coffee.

"We?"

"Yeah. You, Sandy, and me."

"Okay, whatever. Look, Sandy and I are going to Hattiesburg to buy a few things. That is, if that check of yours is any good."

"Oh, it's good all right. What are you going to buy?" J. Marcus asked.

"A bull, some cows, and a johnboat for that pond."

"Oh, that pond! I once hooked Sam Brinson's glasses and slung them right off his head. I thought that man was going to kill me right then and there. He began to beat me over the head with his fishing pole."

"What did you do?" Jon asked.

"I jumped out of the boat and swam my butt back to the bank. Then I ran off with his daughter the very next weekend and married her just across the Alabama state line." J. Marcus laughed at the memory. "Of course, it was quite a while before I was allowed back on this property, let alone fish in that pond again."

"Sandy," Jon yelled, "you getting ready?" Jon already knew the answer.

Minutes earlier, he heard the cartoons blaring from the television set in the living room.

"Tell me about Cassidy."

"Not much to tell. I met her around Christmas."

"Eleanor says she thinks there's more to it than that," J. Marcus continued.

"Maybe, maybe not."

"You are not planning on leaving this place, are you?"

"I don't think so."

"Eleanor said you wouldn't leave. I thought you would be glad to get out of here. I sure the heck was—" J. Marcus almost cursed but was able to stop as Sandy entered the room.

"I'm ready," Sandy declared.

"Brush your teeth?"

"Nope." Sandy stomped back to the bathroom.

"What time is it?" J. Marcus asked because he couldn't find a clock anywhere in the kitchen.

"Quarter till nine. Why?"

"I am expecting something at nine," the elder man said.

They could see Sam approaching on his four-wheeler. Minutes later, Evie and the doc drove up, followed by a long-stretch limousine. Everyone waited as the man in a business suit exited the limo and made his way up to the porch. J. Marcus extended his hand first.

"Bud. Good to see you. Glad you were able to come today. I know how busy you are and all."

"Let's get this over with."

The judge was all business. He had been a friend to Sam Brinson, and he was entrusted with the Brinson will.

"Who is Sam and who is Jon?" the judge asked.

"I'm Sam." Sam looked at Evie and the doc.

"I'm Jon. What's this about?"

"Hold your horses." The judge paused, looking at Jon. "My God, you look just like Sam Brinson when he was young and stupid."

"Get to the best part, judge. I've got a plane to catch," J. Marcus hurried him along.

"Always ready to get out of here," Evie added.

"Would you two shut up? If it weren't for you, this matter would have been settled years ago," the judge said. Then he continued, "To my two grandsons, I leave you each one-half of my land to be given to you after you have good sense in your heads and not before the age of twenty-one."

"What?" both boys said in unison.

"You boys each inherent five hundred acres of Daddy's land." Evie wiped a tear.

"But what about you, Momma?" Sam asked.

"Oh, I did just fine. Granddaddy took care of me just fine," she assured them all.

113

"The deeds have been taken care of. All you boys need to do is sign here, and I'll get back to my retirement."

The judge soon departed. Evie and the doc left, as Sam went to tell Caroline the news. Jon sat at the kitchen table in disbelief. He turned to his father. "Anything else?"

Sandy asked, "Does that mean we can still buy that bull?"

"You may want to wait until that shipment comes in," J. Marcus informed.

"Hey, look at that!" Sandy noticed the eighteen-wheeler coming down the gravel road, kicking up dust as high as the eyes could see.

"Looks like they are here." J. Marcus clapped his hands together.

"They?" Jon did not know if he could stand any more surprises.

The two eighteen-wheelers were full of the finest Brangus cattle he had ever seen—far better than anything he had ever seen come through the stockyard.

Jon turned to his father for an explanation.

"Your grandfather was a stubborn old man, but he was a good man. It was his dream to have the best cattle farm in Mississippi, and he did for years. He only had the two girls, and they married. Well, they didn't marry farmers. That is why he gave you two boys the land. I want you to carry on his dream, for your momma's sake." He paused. "This is to get you started in the right direction. It's my way of paying the old man back."

The truck driver asked them, "Where do you want the bull?"

Out of the back of the trailer walked the biggest bull they had ever seen.

Sandy looked up at Jon. "Do you think the fence will hold him?"

"I better ask Henry."

"Henry is gone, son," the father reminded his son.

"I better ask—" Jon tried again.

"Go with your gut, son. Go with your gut."

"Well, Sandy, looks like we got some work to do."

For the first time, Jon would be acting on his own two feet—nobody giving him directions, nobody but God to stand accountable to.

"Let's put him in the barn, I guess."

It sounded good at the time but later proved to be so wrong. The bull wanted out of the stall during the night, taking half the barn with him. The next morning, the boys woke to chickens scattered throughout the yard and the bull, followed by forty or so cows, standing in the road. The fence he had spent weeks building with Henry had been pushed down in several places. And to make matters worse for Jon, the rooster was in a really bad mood.

CPSIA information can be obtained
at www.ICGtesting.com
Printed in the USA
FSHW02n1350100618
49080FS